A WARRIOR'S PATH

A WARRIOR'S PATH

LANCE BEAR WOLF'S ORIGIN STORY

STEVE STRATTON

For Elle, who lit the Fire.

"Education is your most powerful weapon," Alaxchíia Ahú, Chief
Plenty Coups

CHAPTER
ONE

CROW RESERVATION, MONTANA
1979

The lightning and thunder racing across the plains mark his passing. The torrential rain tries to wash clean my memory of him. He was a good father during the in-between times. When he wasn't hitting us.

I'm surprised he's getting a traditional burial...but I know we follow our traditions for a reason. My mom keeps telling me he's worthy.

I hate the drugs that have taken him and hurt my mother. It runs deep, but I keep it to myself. My father told me the story about the two fighting wolves. The white one is good and the dark one is evil. The one who wins is the one *you* feed. The dark one grows and my anger with it. To my mother I'm full of prayers and forgiveness.

I want revenge... to rid the reservation of his dealer, the man who has caused so much pain, but what can I do? I'm fourteen.

CHAPTER
TWO

CROW RESERVATION, MONTANA, 1981

Time heals all wounds. Alma, my mom, says punching the people who spew stupid sayings won't make me feel better. I can't believe I still get told this crap.

I tried to join the Marine Corps last year, but she wouldn't sign the waiver. She's a teacher and hell bent on my finishing high school.

She deserves better from me. The counselor says I'm acting out and need to let go of my father's death. What she doesn't know is I let him go a long time ago.

His dealer haunts my dreams. I'm stronger and have learned to hunt and kill big game. The dark Wolf tells me Louis Kingman could be next.

It's my sixteenth summer, and I visit our medicine man with a pipe so we can smoke. He tells me to prepare for my vision quest in the sweat lodge. After I purify myself with bear root, my uncle Chayton takes me to Castle Rocks.

There I use an ancient structure to pray and fast for four days. Its opening faces the morning star. Spiritual and enlightening while at the same time grueling and painful.

I learn I can endure. It's during the third night my spirit guide comes to me. Why the Wolf and not the Bear...no one can explain.

I'm different when I return. I visualize the idea of killing Kingman and place it in a lockbox in the corner of my mind. It's time to focus on school. My grades have been C's and a couple of B's until now.

It only takes three months, and I'm on the honor roll.

Don't get me wrong, I'm not in the advanced placement classes. I have history, electronics, metal shop, and auto shop to carry me into this rarefied air.

My mother cries when she sees my grades. "I've always known you could."

Does she know what else hides within me?

In between classes, when I'm not slamming opponents on the wrestling mat, all I think about is becoming a warrior. Our wrestling coach lectures me about my attitude.

"Keep your energy for the matches, Lance. Make sure you treat your training partners and opponents with respect. You won't have any friends or anyone to train with if all you've got to give is anger."

I don't attend other school sports or go to dances. There is a girl I like, and she likes the outdoors like I do. She's super smart and wants to become a wildlife biologist to study wild cats. The bobcat, Canadian lynx, and mountain lion roam the reservation.

I find her a mountain lion and watch her fascination. Turns out she likes to study. I'm about hunting to feed our family. She's not squeamish but prefers science. A couple of hugs, kisses, and laughs, and it's over.

A year later, it's nearing graduation when mom meets Andrew "Call me Andy" Anderson. I like him. He's of Viking stock but educated in American history and Native American studies. He has a grown son who is joining the Army and a daughter doing the same to become a doctor.

He's a warrior from a world away. A Ranger in Vietnam, he teaches me his warrior ethos and parallels to the Crow culture. He chastises me in a joking way about wanting to join the Marine Corps. He doesn't understand my hidden desire to learn how to kill a man.

He takes me on an early season bear hunt. We're seventy-five yards away from the beast when I want to shoot. Andy stops me and whispers. "It's easy to be brave from a distance." An Omaha tribe saying.

We creep closer and stop as the grizzly sniffs the air, but we are down wind. I'm on my hands and knees, moving to an opening where I can kneel and take what Andy calls an ethical shot. He has moved to my left, and I can barely make him out.

I get to the opening and I'm fifteen yards away just as the bear sees my movement. It spins and roars. I pull the trigger. The beast is still coming. As I rise, I chamber another round, there's a gunshot from my left.

I shoot again and slide right to give myself more time to reload. Another gunshot rings out, and the bear's head digs into the loamy dirt.

I'm staring at a grizzly I can touch with the tip of my rifle barrel when Andy appears. "Who taught you to shoot and move?"

"Seemed smart. Not standing in front of a fur-covered locomotive," I say wide-eyed, hands shaking.

"You've got skills and instincts that are hard to teach, Lance. If you want to learn how to kill the drug dealer you despise, join the Army and become a Ranger."

"I don't—"

"It's okay, I've known for a while. Hell, I want to kill him too. But know the hunting of men is wildly different. It doesn't matter if they're a drug dealer or another soldier. Get more experience in life and the art of death before you decide. Once you've killed another man, it will forever change you."

I spend the rest of the time it takes to quarter and pack out the bear thinking. By the time we get home and share the bear with my grandparents and uncles, I've made my mind up.

A week after graduation, I'm on my way to Fort Ord for U.S. Army basic training. The eight weeks in the Monterey area of California aren't exactly easy. I think the marching test is stupid. The field exercises are fun. I take Andy's advice not to make the drill instructors look bad.

Mom and Andy drive down for graduation, and I see them standing as we march onto the parade field. The company commander's speech highlights me as second in my class. Stupid marching test.

Three days later I'm traveling with a classmate, Paul Spann, to the three-week airborne course, aka jump school. We both think we are going to infantry basic first, but the Army has other ideas.

Jump school is a blast, pun intended. Paul and I laugh, get sent to the gig pit, and do hundreds of pushups. My jumps career starts with four C-130 jumps, and a fifth from a C-141.

Andy gets a chuckle out of my time in the pit when he and mom show up for graduation. He asks if I want blood wings, and I of course say yes. It's when a person punches the wings badge and its sharp prongs into your chest. Hence the blood. I think I scared a few of the families with my war cry.

The next day I pack my duffel bag, receive my orders, and move across base to my next training assignment. Paul has a family emergency and must rush home. Before I leave the barracks, one of the senior instructors, a Vietnam vet, surprises me with ancient wisdom from Heraclitus.

"Out of one hundred men, ten shouldn't even be there. Eighty are just targets, nine are the real fighters. We are lucky to have them, for they make the battle. Ah, but the one, one is a warrior, and he will bring the others back."

I take a warrior's mindset with me to the basic infantry course.

THREE

FORT BENNING, GEORGIA

Chayton and Andy taught me to stalk, stay hidden, and keep quiet. This school teaches a different method, and it's called movement to contact. Stealth may be involved a little. But the idea is to find the enemy, make contact and destroy them with overwhelming fire power.

As a Crow, I see parallels to how my people and other tribes attacked from horseback. Still, it seems to lack the finesse of infiltrating an enemy camp before the attack.

But it has history on its side from WWI, WWII, and Korea. From what I know of the Vietnam war, it met with success. But as my uncles have told me, we won many battles and still lost. The generals leading the war couldn't adapt to the style fighting of the Viet Cong and North Vietnamese.

The number one thing I take away from the training is team. It's about you and your teammates supporting each other.

The other thing I notice is all the petty drug dealers and users I see around the base. The guys who drink to much and smell nasty at first formation on Mondays are easy to understand. Our morning runs cure what ails them. I hear them puking at the back of the run formation.

Maybe I'm hypersensitive to drugs and especially people who are high. I saw a lot of it from my dad and his loser friends. Out of one hundred and ninety-two students there appear to be four I can identify as drug users.

Three more I put into the likely bucket. Are they addicted and can't stop? They're stupid and I hate what they are doing. But I realize I need to learn more about addiction.

Despite being a bit of a loner, I like Army life. And I'm now focused on becoming a Ranger like Andy. He's marrying my mom over Christmas. I'm able to get a three-day pass to join in the celebration. Now he's my stepfather, and for reasons I don't fully understand, I want him to be proud of me.

I graduate top of my infantry basic class, but my parents can't make the graduation. They are helping an uncle at his ranch while he recovers from a horse falling on him.

Andy reminds me that during Ranger school I will face a crucible of pain and suffering. What I do with it will determine if I become a warrior or drop out. Little do I know I'm about to be tested and stretched farther than I ever imagined.

The Ranger Indoctrination Program known as RIP is one long crushing physical training session. After dinner, I help other guys with their land navigation skills. I'm positive they will prove valuable to all of us in the days to come.

The three-phase Ranger course is a dazed blur of indeterminate activities, mixed with hyper-focused time on target hacks. There are occasionally funny and exciting, aka dangerous, moments. The simulated operations and real stress combine with little food and sleep to wear me down.

Designed to test your ability to function and lead at the limits of your physical and mental capacity, it's light-years beyond what I experienced during my vision quest. By the time we graduate, my weight loss is severe. I look like a little kid in his dad's uniform.

Ranger school is the first time I ever go sixty-plus days without talking to my parents. Alma and Andy attend the graduation, and he gets to pin my Ranger tab, much to his enjoyment. I spend the next week at home.

My mom put a hand on my arm. "Lance, slow down. There's plenty more food. What did they do to you?"

My stepdad shakes his head and chuckles. "It's not what they did, dear. It's what they don't do. Am I right?"

"Yes, sir. That's the truth," I say pulling up my shirt.

My mom's hand went to her forehead. "Lance Bear Wolf! You are skin and bones."

"One meal a day for weeks at a time," I say. Andy and I high five. Mom blows air between her teeth. "Men."

We talk while sharing meals. Otherwise, I'm sleeping or in my favorite place, the woods. I need to get my strength back before reporting to 2nd Ranger Battalion at Fort Lewis, Washington.

We drive into Crow Agency. Montana. It's our capital for the reservation and I see him, Kingman. I growl and clench my hands into white knuckled fists. My blood rises out of my chest into my neck and face. My breathing is rapid and shallow.

My mind's eye flashes different scenarios. Up close. From a distance. With a knife. With an improvised explosive. My stepfather is driving. I'm up front, and mom is in the back seat.

"We need to talk, Lance. Andy, head to the quiet spot we like by the river," Mom said.

He nods and heads out of town. We drive out past Billy Redfish's place and park under the trees. Mom gets out and strolls down to the water. I follow her, hearing Andy a discreet distance behind.

I catch up with her, and she puts an arm around my shoulders. Here comes the lesson.

"There is a saying in the Al-Anon rooms - '*holding a resentment is like drinking the poison and waiting for the other person to die,*'" she said.

She's taught me to always be honest. I sigh and tell her my truth. "It's a lot more than resentment. He killed my father, a member of our family and tribe. I like the eye for an eye principle here."

"Ah, Lance… revenge has never been and never will be the correct path. It's easy to assign blame to a drug dealer. But what about your father's part in his own death? It pains me to say it… at the end of his life he loved heroin more than you or me. He loved it more than life itself."

Tears flow as I clench my teeth. I gently remove my mother's arm and sit on a rock. The truth sucks. He doesn't belong on a superficial pedestal, certainly not for the in-between times. His demons ate his dreams alive. Demons who seemed real to his drug altered mind.

I search Andy's eyes. They are on fire. His jaw set for retribution.

My mother's soft eyes and my sense of her soul seems conflicted. "Don't let the darkness consume you like it did your father, Lance. Justice will be served when the time is right."

There it is. The answer. Let go of my hatred, but never forget. Put away my "if not now, when" thinking for justice at the right time.

Is it the breeze wafting down the river or my body's reaction to letting go? I'm not sure, but my mom seems pleased by what she senses. I stand and hug her. "Come on you, guys. Let's get something to eat, I'm starving," Alma Nighthawk Bear Wolf said.

"Sounds good to me," I say, seeing the nod from Andy.

We dine on elk, root vegetables, and house salads. Good food fueling my body and soul. I spend one more day with my parents and head to Fort Lewis. I've got a lot more learning to do and need to prove myself worthy of a position in 2nd Ranger Bat as it's called.

The training tempo is intense, and I set aside my hatred for the man who sold poison to my father. But I don't forget.

CHAPTER
FOUR

FORT LEWIS, WASHINGTON

Being the new guy, I'm the lowest of low in our nine-man rifle squad. I spend my first three months learning the Ranger way while pretending to be a gopher. As in, go for this, go for that. The lieutenant needs ABC. The platoon sergeant said, don't listen to the LT, we need XYZ.

I also don't detect illicit drug use. Sure, guys get drunk on the weekend, but even it seems to be tempered by the always ready to deploy mentality.

The President of the United States has US Army units like the 82nd Airborne Division, the 10th Mountain Division, and the Ranger Regiment who can deploy in 72hrs or less. The ready to deploy battalion sized units are on a pre-determined cycle within each command.

The cycle is simple and divides the year into thirds. At 2nd Bat, we are at the bottom of the schedule in our individual training cycle. 1st Bat is in pre-deployment training where they train as individual companies and a battalion and certify they are combat ready.

3rd Bat is in the ready to deploy cycle where they continue to train but remain ready to deploy a company in 24 hours or less and the rest of the Bat in 72hours.

Regardless of deployment cycle status, the company commander and the senior Non-Commissioned Officers, NCOs keep us ready to go, and I like it.

A week later, I'm with our platoon radio operator scrounging all over Fort Lewis for PRC-77 batteries. We're begging, trading, and in one case appropriating batteries for the radio we call the prick-77. We're not sure why, but there's rumors about Lebanon.

When I look deeper, I see the world is on fire. There's the assassination attempt on the South Korean president. A coup of sorts in Grenada. And there's more than a dozen small-scale wars throughout Africa and South America.

Unknown to me, the Joint Chiefs give the execution order on 22 October 1983. A day later we fly to Pope Air Force Base next to Fort Bragg. We are in the air when we hear about the attack on the marine barracks in Beirut.

But we're not headed to Lebanon, our mission is to rescue students held in Grenada who are caught up in the communist infighting. Many on our aircraft want to divert to Beirut for payback.

When we arrive at Pope, they designate us an element of Combined Joint Task Force 123, and we start detailed planning. The maps are black and white printouts.

We do what we can and make a sand table for our section of the operation. It includes dirt, pine needles, twigs, sticks, and tongue depressors. A sand table is a box with sand or dirt used to depict a three-dimensional model of the area of operations or a specific target.

Ours is based on Grenada's Point Salines airport. It brings it home for me, we are going to war.

We are planning what is called a forced entry into a hostile area. Intel says well-trained Cubans are defending our parachute drop zone.

My pucker factor is high, and I try to not show my nervousness. Because of the culture I grew up in, it's not fear of death— okay, a little for sure. What really consumes me is the idea of letting my squad down and getting a teammate killed.

Our mission is to secure the north end of the runway with one other platoon. It's just after midnight when we fly to Hunter Army Airfield at Fort Stewart, Georgia and wait.

After a surprisingly short wait, we are heading south. The plan has us jumping at night, but there is a delay. Scuttlebutt says there is a navigation malfunction on the lead C-130.

I sing my death song on the plane and ask my spirit guide for courage in the upcoming battle.

Today is a good day to die
I grieve for those left behind
I ask that you keep fear from my heart
Give me strength and if it's my time
Let me honor my family and my people

It's light when we jump, and I thank the creator that I'm not standing in the door to see how low we are. We jump at 0545 from 500 feet to get under the anti-aircraft weapons the Cubans are shooting at us.

It is the shortest parachute ride I've ever taken. Rounds snap by while I descend. I just miss a chunk of broken concrete, one of many strewn around runway to keep us from landing aircraft. As I shuck off my parachute harness, I breathe in the odors of combat.

Spent gunpowder and debris from anti-aircraft and mortar rounds hang in the air. It takes a beat to realize one of the many sounds I hear is bullets aimed at me.

I run to catch up with my teammates, and we move under fire in what's called bounding. One squad moves forward and establishes a base of fire on the enemy. Then the second squad moves ahead and does the same for the first.

We support each other, making the Cubans hide when we light them up. At the other end of the runway, I can see our brothers battling armored personnel carriers.

We overwhelm the soldiers around the airport and take more than two hundred prisoners. By 0900, we have rescued 138 students.

I'm on point as we head to our secondary objective, the library at a remote campus where a student said the rest are being held.

We're moving down the hallway, a silent train of death. I reach the door and hold, waiting for the signal to go.

An armed soldier my age steps out and screams as he brings his weapon up. I hesitate a heartbeat then shoot him at point-blank range. I'm not trained to lead an assault, so I tackle him out of the way to clear the door for my teammates.

I jump to my feet and stare at the man I've just killed. I'm not sure what to think. Should I have tackled and disarmed him versus taking his life? Could I have? He's within a year or two of my age, and I've ended his life.

My head is spinning when I hear several more shots ring out. I race inside to hear calls of all clear. Right away, I'm checking to make sure soldiers aren't hiding in the students.

Several of the kids smell like they are sweating weed. I wrinkle up my nose and shake my head at the thought they want to be doctors.

We are holding the kids, most of them older than me, for a Caribbean unit called OECS. Meanwhile, my personal hero, General Schwarzkopf, is trying to get U.S. Army helicopters.

But we end up with four Marine Sea Stallions to evacuate them. Students taken care of; we patrol back south to Point Salines airport to await our transportation home. We have done our job and done it well.

Later in the afternoon, a group of Cuban soldiers are led by us on the way to their holding area. I hear a yell "Grenade!" As it rolls toward us, I tackle my platoon sergeant, protecting his body with mine. The explosion flash burns through my eyelids, and my ears ring like never before.

I blink my eyes and self-assess. I'm leaking, but nothing major. I'm lucky.

My platoon sergeant must be barking at me. His lips are moving, and he's waving his hands. All I hear is ringing. He's talking and pointing at me. I'm in shock from being blasted and not feeling a thing. It's still in effect when our medic arrives. I complain I hate drugs and don't want them. Through the ringing I hear him call me a dumbass. He stabs me with morphine.

I've been in the Army for less than a year. If this keeps up, I'm not going to make it to ten.

CHAPTER
FIVE

FORT LEWIS, WASHINGTON

After a short stay in the Fort Stewart hospital, I'm back at my platoon. I'm handed combat awards and told I'm being sent to the primary leadership development course.

When I graduate top student, I have fifteen months in service. The company and battalion commanders sign a waiver, and I'm promoted to E-4 Corporal.

My squad leader, who is an E-6 staff sergeant, reminds me not to get a big head. He tells me to keep working to be the best I can be. The next ninety days of training are conventional and boring.

We're at the range a lot. My squad leader lets me team up with the snipers, where I learn a ton about long-distance shooting.

I like the idea of being a sniper. It suits my silent stalking mentality and skills. I investigate the sniper course, but there aren't any slots for the next seven months.

An opportunity to attend the Colombian Army Lancero school works its way through the system, and I volunteer.

I'm excited for the opportunity. I've always been interested in the history and peoples of the Americas. A Ranger captain named Puckett designed the Lancero training in coordination with a Colombian, Major Bernal, back in 1956.

All I've been told is it's hard and soldiers get hurt attempting the course. Oh yeah, and it's eleven days longer than Ranger school.

It's another month and a half before I get orders to the course. In the meantime, I get the Latin American Headstart Program cassettes and start leaning Spanish.

Two days after I get my orders, I fly commercial from Seattle to Houston and then Houston to Bogota, Colombia. I wear a baseball cap, so my high and tight haircut doesn't call me out as a weirdo extremist. It's late afternoon when I exit the plane.

"Wolf!" A guy yells from across the concourse as I'm heading towards the terminal door. I turn to find a well-tanned, good-looking guy who looks like a wealthy tourist rather than a military liaison. He reaches out a hand and I shake it.

"Thadeus Morgan. You can call me Gus. Follow me," he says and spins on a heel and heads for the door. We jump into a Jeep, and head into town.

As we're driving, he interrogates me in a nice, easy manner. It gets me talking and thinking.

We switch roles, and I learn he's a staff sergeant medic. He is one of the original fifteen Green Berets who deployed to El Salvador in 1981. Turns out Morgan hasn't been stateside since and has stayed in South America switching between El Salvador, Colombia, and Peru.

"How do you keep from getting ordered back to the states?" I ask.

He smiles his Hollywood best and avoids the question. "If you're looking for emeralds, I've got a contact. If you interested in the beautiful women, I'm your guy."

We stop at a house, and he jumps out. "Come on, this is where you'll stay for the night. Lana, the housekeeper is also the cook, and she's excellent."

I follow him by a guard with a double-barreled shotgun.

Double-barrel shotgun?

Inside the house, I smell a combination of savory odors as he shows me to a room.

"Drop your bag. Let's eat."

My first hour in in Colombia, and I'm having an authentic dinner.

My new friends include a Special Forces medic, a housekeeper, and to my surprise two amazing looking Colombian women.

Morgan introduces them. "Wolf, this is Isabella and Daniela. You can call them Issy and Danny. Ladies, this is Lance Bear Wolf. He's a real American Indian."

"Like in the cowboy movies?" Issy asked.

"Yes, and I take scalps for trophies," I say, joking.

The ladies screech. Morgan laughs. "He's kidding. Let's eat."

The meal is called bandeja paisa. There is pork, rice, beans, ground meat, chorizo, fried eggs, avocado, sauces, and a bunch more I don't know, but it all tastes great. After dinner, it's a dessert called tres leches cake and coffee.

During the dinner Morgan tells us several "no shit there I was" stories. He has the girls giggling. He's got me to thinking he's crazy but would do anything to save a teammate.

I've hardly gotten a word in edgewise, but the ladies seemed impressed that I am trying to speak their native language An hour later it's time to go out, and I decline and head back to my room and language tapes.

The time is branded into my memory. At 0210, the sound of multiple automatic weapons fire and racing cars outside my bedroom window has me jumping like a cat touching aluminum foil. I roll to the floor thrashing for the pistol Morgan slipped me.

I still have the cassette player headset on, and now it's twisted around my throat. I rip it away and remember the pistol is on the nightstand. I grab it from my place on the floor and press check there is a round in the chamber. Outside tires squeal and there is shouting.

By the time I'm ready there's a lull in the shooting as the vehicles burn rubber and race by the house. The shooting continues down the road.

It takes deep breathing to settle down and fall back to sleep. Later I feel a woman join me in bed. It's Danny. I put my arm around her and enjoy another three hours of sleep.

CHAPTER
SIX

BOGOTA, COLOMBIA

I wake up at 0530, stretch then meditate. I'm in a country best known for illegal drugs like weed and cocaine. The Colombian Army prosecutes an on-again, off-again drug war while at the same time waging war on anti-government guerrillas.

I don't expect to see any use at the Lancero school, but it should be all around us. I hope we run into a lab to destroy or a supply chain to disrupt. I know I need a lot more training, but I really want to get after it.

Later after breakfast with the best coffee I've ever experienced, Morgan takes me back to the airport. I board a Colombian Air Force CASA C-212 for the short flight to the School of Lanceros in Tolemaida. It's 120 kilometers south-southwest of Bogota.

Right away, I sense my limited language skills are going to be a problem. I'm the only American assigned to my squad, but the Colombians are cool. There is one first corporal, the US equivalent of a sergeant, who outranks me. From what I gather, he has counter-drug combat experience.

The rest are newbie privates. There is one instructor who speaks limited English, words versus sentences. But I'll take what I can get.

It only takes a heartbeat to recognize everyone else has shaved their heads, instructors included. I stumble through asking to borrow an old electric razor to remove what little hair I have on top.

We start with a PT test, and I max it out. But I come in second in the run. The guy ahead of me isn't breathing hard at all. I find out later he's Paez, which is one of Colombia's native American tribes from the Andes. Good kid.

They issue us Galil rifles and Colombian MREs and tell us to get ready for inspection. We lay all our kit out on the parade field.

We spend the rest of the day doing pushups and running around our formation. After five hours of the instructors finding something wrong with everyone's gear, the training starts.

The first phase, two weeks and a couple of days long, is very basic, for me at least. Weapons, infantry, and ranger-like tactics. When we're not practicing what we've just learned, we are running and doing pushups.

If one guy messes up, we all pay. Everything is on a points system and is graded at the squad level. We can all get them, or all lose them based on how we perform as a team. The only time it's individual is during every other day PT tests.

There are two things I notice right away. One, the instructors will lay hands on you if you're messing up. Two, is an almost total disregard for safety. It's most apparent on the obstacle course.

A student falls off every time. Most of the time it's a sprained ankle or bruised shoulder. One Colombian broke his leg.

At the end of the phase, I've probably lost a dozen pounds. The Colombian MREs are high in sugar versus protein. We get a tortilla and sausage with rice for breakfast. Not having the longer-lasting energy from protein will be a problem in the long run.

We board trucks for mountain phase. Before we leave, they hand out two banged-up and scratched red painted magazines of live ammo for each of us. The story is there are quasi-guerrilla groups and narcos who transit the area.

We will carry live rounds, as will the instructors. We will have to be careful when we aggress against each other to make sure we are shooting blanks. I worry about the newbies.

Each squad is told to secure one of the black pots. We also take the equivalent of a five-pound bag of rice, and a five-pound bag of pasta. Everyone carries cans of tuna and sardines. No resupply: we carry this with us all the time.

At the mountain site, I know the knots, how to create expedient harnesses and set secure ropes. The rest of the guys are new to mountaineering the army way. My Paez teammate, Sebastian, is like a mountain goat and has only used ropes to tie bundles on his llama.

Like first phase, this is one place where I can help the squad, and we score high. The rock we rappel from is not dangerous and the anchors look solid. I tie in Australian style and come down face first with my ruck on and rifle in front like I'm assaulting.

The instructors take advantage of my showing off and make me do it again with a teammate over my back. Sebastian is the lightest and laughs as I balance him on my back.

I run down the cliff as fast as I can, the rope burning through my glove. Much higher than normal, I apply tension, the rope stretches, and we thunder in. At the last second, I remember to extend my arm, so I don't get a face full of rifle.

But it's not far enough, and the front sight tears my cheek right below my eye. We're alive and laughing. We get to do a hundred pushups and my eye swells shut. My squad starts calling me pirate or sea wolf, I can't tell which.

Every day right before 1600 it rains hard. The rocks are slick, the ropes are slick.

We're slipping and banging on the rock. It sucks! But I haven't broken anything yet. When we're not on the rocks, we practice patrolling.

The next day, the final test is a vertical assault up a cliff face to the target, a simulated narco lab site. There are Colombian regular army soldiers helping the instructors, and they've built a multi-building compound.

An instructor provides a hand-drawn map and puts together two squads. I'm assigned the command of the operation. The regular army guys roleplay the narcos.

Before we launch, I make sure my squad and the others are using blanks. All the live rounds are in our rucksacks.

Four minutes after I initiate the assault, I do a quick headcount and move off to the simulated extraction point. We hand over the intel and are told to head to another point and set up for the night. Before we move out, the newly appointed squad leaders switch everyone back to live ammo.

The next morning, we patrol out to a dirt road to trucks.

We're halfway through.

We drive for a long time. We've gained altitude, and it rains on us. This becomes the new normal, and there is no drying out.

My feet are wrinkly, and I'm worried about trench foot.

Jungle phase. It's all new to me. I'm used to the forests of the mountain states. There's minimal training. After teaching us how to safely cross water, it's mostly odd stuff like snakes, electric eels, and spiders. They're everywhere.

The rest of the time it's patrol, patrol, patrol, operation planning and simulated attacks. I wear my wet socks around my neck and waist to get them dry. After a heavy rain, the temperature change causes hypothermia. My teeth chatter like they're going to break.

With the rain is mud and more mud. We do live fire exercises, and I shout to stay online so we don't shoot each other.

I'm banged up, bleeding and more tired than at Ranger school. I haven't been counting days; I take it as it comes. I'm surprised when we're handed escape and evasion maps, a survival-type radio, and three more mags of live rounds.

The instructors take all our training ammo, then give us a two-minute warning order.

My Spanish has grown during the course as has my ability to understand what my teammates and the instructors are saying. "You are the only survivor after the guerillas ambushed your squad. You must use everything you've learned to make it to your pickup point. We will insert you by truck. You have five days, or you fail."

Escape and evasion, five days. I look at the map and realize my route is through the Amazon district on the border with Ecuador. As soon as I'm dropped off, I haul ass to get distance.

But it's not like I get to sprint across a field. It's super thick, and a third of the time I'm on my hands and knees.

We've been told to radio our approach to the waypoint locations and acknowledge that we have retrieved the coordinates. I'm not about to tell anyone I'm near a waypoint. I wait until I've been at the waypoint and I'm two hundred meters away.

Three days later while resting up in a tree, I realize I've not seen or smelled drugs since starting the course. I didn't expect I would, but I thought it possible with the regular army guys.

I set the thought aside as I head to the second to last waypoint. I'm as stealthy as a jaguar in my head when they rush me.

I have my hand in the box to retrieve the coordinates for the next waypoint when I hear their boots thundering across the plank floor. They are wearing ballistic helmets with night vision.

I dislocate my right thumb when it gets stuck in a pair of night vision goggles as I use the soldier's energy to slam him against the wall.

Crap, it's bound to be my turn.

CHAPTER
EIGHT

ESCAPE AND EVASION TRAINING, COLOMBIA

I fight back short of causing severe injury to the instructors and think about ripping off live rounds to stop them in an attempt escape.

Nah, bad idea. Better to pass than win.

There's a clang noise a millisecond before I black out. When I wake, my head hurts. Dang, my whole-body hurts.

I scratch caked mud and blood out of my eyes.

Now I know why I'm so flipping cold.

I'm naked laying on bamboo.

Holy crap! I'm in a bamboo cage.

I'll deal with the physical side of being a POW, but I'm concerned with the mental games I've heard they will play.

My vision and thinking are clearing, so I take stock of my situation and resources. Laughing hurts but helps my morale. There's a bucket in the corner of the cage.

It smells like roadkill baking inside a Florida dumpster on a hot August day.

While I'm checking out the room, the door opens. A guard who wears solid green slides sloppy rice into my cage. More rice. I'm so tired of rice.

I may never eat it again after this course. I want to wipe my hand off, but it's just bamboo and me. And I'm filthy.

Never mind. Just eat. Ah… man, weevils. I've seen them before at my grandparents, in corn grandpa said we shouldn't leave open. He picked them out, and we ate the corn after grandma washed and rehydrated it.

There's meat; it looks like pork. It's not a big portion, and smells awful, but I gulp it down anyway. Just when I'm sitting back and feeling like I've got this, a couple of goons appear and yank me from the cage.

I don't struggle, just the opposite. They put a black hood over my head and drag me to another building. It has an AC unit pretending to be a meat locker chiller.

They tie me to a cold metal chair. In seconds my teeth are chattering. I hear the hose and know it's not going to be warm.

I'm on the verge of breaking my own bones. The water is glacial. I'm waiting for the progression. Then it stops. Then a fan starts blowing a gale force wind at the same time as the music starts.

Knuckleheads are playing Motorhead's "Iron Fist." I start rocking out to the song. Oh, oh, you forgot to secure my legs. I'm giddy as I jump to my feet and sprint backwards, like a free safety, as fast as I can.

I'm back in the cage when I wake up. I feel as if I'm wrapped in a cocoon of pain. My eyes water, the smell is terrible. I realize I'm lying in my excrement. My stomach churns. I vomit and explode.

Guards come out of nowhere and hose me down. I crawl forward and put my back to the guards. The cold water feels luxurious. The numbness it provides, priceless.

I'm using the sun and the shadows it casts to keep track of relative time. For all I know it's faked. It really doesn't matter. There's only survival. For one more hour. One more minute… one more breath.

Here we go again. This time there's no bag over my head, and I take in the compound as I'm manhandled to another building. I hear voices in the distance but can't make out what they're saying. I'm tied to a wooden chair with arm rests.

I spend the rest of the day with my new friend Soto. He's my buddy, the good cop. A young woman using the name Tayna is the bad cop. She makes fun of my manhood in creative ways to embarrass and anger me.

I make up stories, and when she figures out my teammates are a lie, they bring in the heavy hitter. He's an older guy called Mister X. They tell me his bio. It includes being held for several months by the FARC.

I whisper to myself. "Those are his cages... this is going to suck."

CHAPTER
NINE

ESCAPE AND EVASION TRAINING, COLOMBIA

I've got zero energy left to fight. X ties me up and makes me squat with my hands behind me. I remember seeing this in a manual Andy kept from his days in Vietnam. I have a second of appreciation for its creativeness.

Suddenly, he yanks my arms up and I experience a new level of pain, I scream, then catch my breath. When I do, I laugh and get punched.

I'm surprised Mister X knows stuff about me. He's making it personal by using my biological father's history to fire me up. I snarl and keep laughing between cursing them. Soto punches me to sleep.

I wake up in the jungle with my teammates. I've got my ragged uniform on, and I'm being manhandled through the bush.

There's a clearing ahead, and I hear a helicopter. I'm tossed on board, and the helicopter surges into the azure sky. It's cold and I pull my bare feet into my chest. Sebastian asked what I did to receive such treatment, and I don't have an answer.

When we get back to Tolemaida, they tell us we get four hours to clean up and be ready to move out. No equipment required.

I tell my teammates to shower first. I'm going to use all the rest of the hot water. I take a hand full of Motrin and soak in the shower until the hot water is gone.

Three hours later an instructor yells for us to fall out. We line up, and a Colombian officer I take to be the Lancero school commander pins on our badge and salutes us. After he leaves, we congratulate each other, and I see Morgan step out of his jeep.

"What'd yah think, Wolf?"

"Don't need to do it again," I say.

"True. Once is enough. But now you've got instant credibility when you come back."

"Are Special Forces medic slots hard to get?" I ask, intrigued.

"No. But make sure you demand assignment to 7th Group, or you could end up in Africa."

"Roger that."

"Let's head to Bogota. You've got two days until you need to report back to your unit. In the meantime. I'll show you how we're supporting the president's counter-drug focus on the Medellin cartel. Oh, yeah, Danny's waiting."

UNITED STATES EMBASSY,
BOGOTA, COLOMBIA,
MARCH 1984

The circle in front of the embassy makes it seem like an up-scale hotel. Until you look past the palm trees and drop-off area. The thick steel gate sits between the three-foot thick and fifteen-foot-high security walls.

Morgan drove around the circle and headed for the employee entrance. "Use this entrance when you come back. I'll make sure they have a badge for you," he said handing me a temporary badge.

We stopped at a guard shack and presented our badges.

"You better head in. Your colonel friend is a couple of cars behind you," the Marine guard said.

"Roger that," Morgan said and drove through gate, taking the first open parking spot. "Come on, let's go before the idiot jacks us up."

He must not be on the best terms with the officer.

We scurry, just short of a run, into the embassy. I keep track of the turns when Morgan retrieves another badge from his pocket and swipes it at a door. He pulls me inside and smiles like a Cheshire cat.

"What's that about?"

He shakes his head and pushes me into a side room and closes the door. "The deputy commander of the military attaché section thinks I spend too much time with the DEA."

"What do you like about working with DEA?"

"As Special Forces we train the Colombians, so they are ready to hunt guerrillas and narcos. It's a strategic mission, but boring. Working with the DEA and their Colombian partners gets me in the field on actual operations where I can make a difference."

"So, you're a war junkie and need to be in a fight?" I ask, thinking I know the answer.

"No! My younger brother got high on cocaine and killed himself and my mother in a car accident. I want to hurt the cartels anyway I can."

I can sense his fury. It's in his narrow eyes and fists. I know this hatred firsthand.

"Let's go to my desk, and I'll show you what this team is doing about it," Morgan said.

The rest of the day he shows me DEA reports. They highlight the tons of cocaine coming into the US a month. The cartel profits are staggering. America is ramping up its support for the drug war.

There are plans for more Special Forces training missions to support the militaries and national police forces of Bolivia, Chile, Peru, Ecuador, and, of course, Colombia.

We are out for lunch when a guy with shifty eyes steps in front of us.

"Wolf, this is Jose. No, it's not his real name. What's up?"

"We're a go. Bring him with you. We'll need all the shooters we can get," Jose said, then turned and ambled away.

"Dude, what's up with him?"

"Wrong question, young padawan. We must visit the security specialist. What clearance to do you have?"

"Secret, why?"

"You're now part of the biggest raid of the drug war," he said, a gleam in his eyes.

"But my orders. I'll be AWOL if I don't—"

"Don't worry. I'll have my guy in the military section extend you for a week. This will be epic. You don't want to miss this one."

Oh, man, I've just been co-opted as the sorcerer's apprentice... what the heck, it's a chance to hurt a drug cartel.

I fill out paperwork and receive the briefing. I have a temporary badge, and snap, I'm a part of the DEA task force in Colombia. We head into a room he says is a Secure Compartmented Information Facility. To me, it's just a conference room with a thick door and flashing lights.

"What makes this conference room a S-C-I-F?"

"It's shielded. Nothing gets in or out once the door is closed."

I'm wide-eyed and wondering what's coming next.

CHAPTER
ELEVEN

AMERICAN EMBASSY BOGOTA, COLOMBIA

Morgan walks over to a series of stitched-together pictures lying on top of a table-size map and points. "This is where we are going at 0100, Tranquilandia. We'll fly CASA to Nevia, then switch for the last two hours and assault in Blackhawks from the 160th."

I lean over the map and circle the pictures with my finger. "This is out in the middle of nowhere. How'd you find it?" I ask. I want to know the indicators so I can use them back on the reservation.

"This story starts with a knucklehead approaching a gas company in New Jersey about a large purchase of ether. They use it to process cocaine. The DEA tracked the tanks to Tranquilandia. Can you identify the indications pointing to it being drug lab?" he asked.

"I'm not an intel guy, but this is a runway and here are tracks leading into the jungle. Maybe an airplane. What are these?" I ask, noticing an odd color between the trees.

"Canvas tarps patterned after the brush in the area."

I chuckle and point. "The lab is underneath. I see the outline of barrels. Which ones are the ether?"

"They're not visible. Ether is very volatile. It's likely kept separate until they need it."

"DEA gets lucky and tags the barrels, but most of the time the labs are hard to find, right?" I ask.

"Yes. We look for flights or trucks going in and out of specific locations. Guys flashing a lot of money around. Reports of generator sounds or the odor of chemicals. And we can spot the trash piles the operators create."

"How about a guy or guys buying an odd collection of supplies?"

"Could be, or could be moonshiners, like back home," Morgan said and laughed. "Our job is to provide support to the DEA and Colombian National Police. It will be like your Ranger airport takedown operations. But instead of jumping, we will land right on the improvised runway. Everyone has an AK, and there will be RPGs on site. We advise and assist. If a weapon points at you, drop them."

"Cool. Do we have time for dinner with Issy and Danny?"

"Yeah, let's head to the house and chill before we launch."

The seafood paella is excellent. I love the crispy rice at the bottom. I keep quiet for the first half hour as Morgan works his magic. When I talk, it impresses the girls how much better I speak. I'm making eye contact with Danny when my brother in mayhem drops a bomb, ruining the moment.

He drops his napkin and downs his beer. "Sorry, ladies. We have to go."

Issy's lower lip protrudes like a pouting child. Danny frowns and squeezes my knee.

"Yes, my lovelies. Our idiot colonel demands our attendance at a conference with the Venezuelan ambassador and his security team."

I kiss Danny on the cheek and inhale her essence, then head to the jeep with Morgan. As we drive to the embassy, I lean over. "Why the BS story?" I ask.

"I haven't finished vetting them yet," he said, eyes on the road.

Great, just great. I have the hots for a potential cartel plant.

Five hours later we arrive at Nevia and off-load into chalks, units of guys for each helicopter.

"We're way behind schedule," I say.

"Not to worry, we have added extra time to the plan. As long as we assault before daylight, it's good."

It doesn't surprise me Morgan is part of chalk one on the Alpha bird with the assault team. He tells me he's been working with the unit for a year. He says they are solid.

Chalk two - Bravo will secure the north end of the runway and anything or person they find at the worker's camp. I'm in chalk three - Charlie. Our mission is securing the south end. The chalk four - Delta team will land to the west and secure the route to and dock at the river.

As the helicopters lift off, my earpiece cracks. The encryption adds a choppiness to Morgan's voice. "Stay frosty, Wolf. We're not sure where the security force beds down."

I scan the team, and the policemen appear hard. I'm odd man out in my DEA body armor. Most are pretending to sleep or just don't care.

I'll stay back until I'm sure they won't shoot me by mistake.

They're checking me out. I nod and close my eyes. In my mind, I'm looking at an enormous billboard – WHAT CAN GO WRONG? Then the voiceover starts. "Confusion when we land, missed assignments, lack of muzzle control, freezing up, not stopping the threat before helping a down teammate."

OK, I get it!

I replace the billboard and voice with Danny's image. Long dark hair, dark eyes, full lips. Broad shoulders and attractive curves.

TWELVE

MH-60, PREPARING TO ASSAULT

I awake to the team leader's ten-minutes command and check my M4 rifle is ready and safe. My pistol is still by my side, and I can reach the Randall knife I borrowed from Morgan's collection.

"Five minutes," the major said.

We turn 180 degrees to head north as we descend. At one minute, the cops slide the doors open. The humid jungle air flows in. The policemen are irritated with their fogging googles.

I just squint through the debris and dust from the rotor blade wash as we land. I flip down my night vision goggles and exit last.

My chalk is online as it advances to the south at a fast walk. I want them to run but have to defer to their leader.

They keep online, and their muzzle control is solid as they sweep the jungle to their front and sides.

I react to gunfire from our left front as it cuts down the two nearest cops. I dump rounds into the spot and yell contact left.

The major stops to make sense of what's going on. My training takes over, and I assault through the ambush.

I glance to my right, and two of the cops are with me. I detect a narco trying to flank us and drop him, then empty the rest of my mag at the ambush team. When my rifle locks open I switch to my pistol.

Out of the corner of my eye, I watch a cop let go of his rifle and come up with a grenade. He throws it at the source of the ambush.

I yell "Frag out!" and slide to a stop behind a barrel at the tree line.

Fragmentation pings the barrel. I rise and search for threats. There are four bad guys in an unmoving pile.

I join the two cops and the rest of the team. We enter a tarp-covered jungle home with pots, cots, and mosquito nets.

One of the cops didn't respond in a timely manner to my calling frag out. He has a couple of bites, but nothing life-threatening. The major faces me and pounds my shoulder.

"Loco Lobo," he said, and the cops give me a terrible impression of Hooah. Their leader gets them back on task clearing the sleeping quarters. I step out to the tree line and radio Morgan.

"Alpha one two, Charlie one two, sector clear."

"Roger that, Charlie one two. Report to my pos."

When I walk into the central lab, which has light, I flip up my night vision. Gus is standing with the DEA lead and the commander of the national police unit.

"What's up?" I ask.

He points to a map. "I count nine other locations. It's a lot of product we can stop before it heads to America."

"Outstanding. How can I help?"

Morgan glances at the DEA lead and police commander, who nod their concurrence. "We did not train the police in night patrolling. We'll consolidate our current positions and after first light you'll lead a team to this cluster. Haul whatever product you can back here and destroy the rest.

Just before noon the next day, Morgan appears and slaps my shoulder. "Loco Lobo has a nice ring to it. It will stand out in my report to 2nd Battalion," he said, then belly laughed. "The National Police want to give you an award for bravery."

"On man, no, please. I'm already going to be the target of so much crap."

"Don't BS me, you love it. You saved the team and punished the world's largest cartel. Even the President of the United States calls them enemy number one. Wait until the ambassador tells the president. You'll be at the White House."

"I admit I enjoy hurting the cartel just as much as you do—"

"Why?" Morgan asked, staring at me his eyes slits.

I sigh and scan the area to make sure no one else is listening. "My biological father died from a heroin overdose. I've wanted to kill the dealer since I was fourteen. My stepfather told me to join the Army to gain experience before deciding what to do," I say, and stare back at Morgan. "Now, I know my path."

The rest of the Tranquilandia operation is clean-up. The police capture forty-plus workers from the jungle. The bigwigs crow to the press about their success.

I say goodbye to my team and receive a, "see you next time", reponse. I will be back, but when I do it will be as a Special Forces medic.

Two more years as a Ranger and I'll have the experience everyone wants me to have. Then I'll put my papers in for selection.

We hop on a Colombian helicopter back to Nevia and then the CASA back to Bogota. I expect Morgan to be in sales mode, but he's quiet.

When we board the CASA, I lean in and speak over the noise of the engines. "I can hear the gears turning. What's up?"

"When you come back, it's just not narcos. There are guerrilla organizations who want to overthrow the Colombian and other governments down here."

I slap Morgan's back. "Well, dang! I can't wait. Sign me up!"

I head back to 2nd Battalion, where I belong. I could have stayed another week but it's the right decision if I don't want my hatred for drugs to become all-consuming. My stepfather cautions me not to hate my enemies for fear that I will become them.

I need a break. Some physical and mental space to figure this out.

It's overcast and forty degrees colder at Fort Lewis. I don't know the guy when I sign in. The company is at the airfield for a night jump and movement to the urban combat training site.

I change clothes and unpack my stuff. I have time to catch up with my squad, put my knees in the breeze, and take part in the training. But our first sergeant flings open the door to the two-man room I share with my squad leader.

"Well, look who it is… the savior of Colombia."

I spin to attention. "Ready to focus on Ranger business."

"Good. The regimental commander and a Colombian big wig will be here tomorrow. Your Class A uniform better be spotless and correct, or I'll have your ass, Wolf."

"Yes, sergeant," I say.

At 1045 the next morning, the company is called to attention. Colombian General Andres Molina pins me with the Colombian Police Star Order and Military Medal of Valor.

Colonel Skroggins , our regimental commander pins me with the Meritorious Service Medal. Then he spends a couple of minutes on our need to maintain our anytime, anywhere readiness posture. As he leaves the podium, he stops before me, and I come to attention. "Anything I can do for you, Ranger?" he asked.

He's one of the best leaders I've ever known. A soldier's soldier, a mustang officer.

"Yes, sir. A tryout for the reconnaissance detachment."

"Done. Take a couple of days to prepare."

"I stay ready, sir!"

"XO, you heard the corporal. Report in the morning, Wolf."

The battalion commander frowns while the company commander suppresses a smile. As they leave the command sergeant major shakes my hand and whispers. "Show-em how it's done, Wolf."

When the formation is dismissed, the guys give me a few "lucky bastard" comments.

I keep my secret weapon, Thadeus aka Gus Morgan, to myself. My squad leader wonders why I want to go through a third assessment having survived two long courses already.

What can I say? It calls to me at an instinctual level, more like a deep attraction. Plus, this will be useful training for my personal fight. They have the latest tech from the DOD and Agency research departments.

THIRTEEN
ATLANTA AIRPORT, GEORGIA

An old Army cadence sums up the next couple of months as I endure yet another selection. *Here we go again same old crap again…*

Guys in civilian clothes pick me up and four others. They drive us down to the Ranger school mountain training site in Dahlonega, Georgia and take us to a secluded section of Camp Merrill.

The first week is physical and mental tests intertwined with interviews. More IQ tests, as if the Army entrance exams don't cut it. Being a tech geek, I know I test well.

The interviews with cadre and the shrink focus on my why. I'm sure my expression gives away my thoughts about my father when the shrink points out he was a loser. I laugh and agree. "Yeah, but like you and me, he was a combination of love and self-hate. I learned valuable skills and what not to do with my life," I say.

"You're one of those silver linings, everything is nice whack-os, aren't you? You must get sad and demoralized when things don't work out," the shrink said.

Oh, damn, I want to mess with this dude. Better not.

"To die for nothing is sad. To live without a purpose is sad. But no one can make me sad without my permission. I never give it," I say with a tight-lipped smile. "I do search for the positive, but I balance it against reality. I celebrate my positive emotions and seek to minimize the effect of destructive emotions like sadness, grief, jealousy, anger, and fear. I believe I'm an unbiased thinker."

"Interesting. Do you consider yourself a stoic?"

"Yes, and I also integrate eastern martial teachings like Sun Tzu and Miyamoto Musashi."

"Do you meditate and enjoy stillness?"

"Yep. Do you know what counting coup is in Native American culture?"

"I think so. It's tasks required to become a warrior or chief, right?"

"It can be, but it's about courage. Do you have the courage to charge an enemy and strike them with your hand, coupstick, or weapon? And are you brave enough not to kill them?"

"You're a decorated combat soldier. Have you counted coup and not killed another combatant?"

"Yes."

"Why didn't you kill them?"

"I could have. It would have been easy, but they posed no threat."

"You decided no threat, but to who, you? What about your team-mates, the mission?"

"Yes, it's what I'm paid to do. Make life and death decisions for my team and myself."

"Well said, Wolf. But we don't need assaulters or door kickers in this job. It's about reconnaissance, not combat."

"Sir let's be real here. First off, you cannot trigger me into saying I like blood lust and death over compassion. I am capable of both, as the situation dictates. I spent the first eighteen years of my life learning how to sneak up on people and animals. How to stay hidden for hours and days. How to kill with primitive weapons and live off the land. How to memorize what I see, smell, hear, and feel while I watch my target. No one in this group of candidates is better."

After a furious bit of scribbling on his notepad, the shrink releases me, and it's right into another long hump. This time, over rugged passes with a sixty-five-pound ruck and thousands of feet of elevation change.

The guy who picked us up is leading, and he's a beast keeping a stiff pace.

It's not tactical and it's not meant to be. This is the weed-out-the-weak phase. Seven days later, I'm carrying one hundred and five pounds in my pack.

I make the checkpoint with time to spare. I'm tired but in high spirits. An instructor hands me new coordinates.

I plot them, I'll arrive to the last of the four at daybreak. This long walk appears to be copied after the Special Air Service version.

No time hack or known distance. Just keep walking, and we will pick you up. I can feel it. Thinking I will be picked up at my final checkpoint is a waste of energy.

If I don't hurt myself, I've got a chance.

CHAPTER
FOURTEEN
NORTH GEORGIA

I trip and slam into the dirt face first. I laugh and roll to a painful knee, then rise using my rifle for help. Upright, I function-check my rifle then swig a long pull from my canteen.

The ache is growing so I resume walking to take my mind off it. I envision myself as a torn-up Pig Pen from Charlie Brown. I laugh and it soothes the pain a touch.

I'm walking in intermittent light and darkness as I follow my compass to the final checkpoint. The sun rises, but it's not high enough to light up the rugged terrain.

A twig crunches, and I take cover and switch my rifle to automatic.

It's Wooden, an instructor. "You're on the long walk. Get up, Wolf."

Blood flushes my beat-up dirty face. Where the heck is my mind at?

"Trying to ambush me?" he asked.

"Gave it some thought," I say, walking up to him.

"How do you like your dirt sandwiches?"

"Bloody."

He suppresses a laugh. "Show me where you are on your map."

I retrieve my map from my cargo pocket, orient it, and take a second to find our location. Then I point. Wooden must intercept candidates at this spot.

Scanning the area, I understand why. He has easy access, and this is the perfect spot to check your position.

His frown lets me know he's disappointed. "You're all banged up. Why don't you come with me? I've got hot coffee, breakfast burritos, and a hot shower."

"Thanks. I've got a checkpoint to make," I say.

"You're good. You don't have anything to prove."

"I do, but thanks, sarge," I say and walk on.

Dude needs to work on his psych game.

It's mid-day when I walk through an area where the instructors are standing around eating barbecue. The smells make my stomach churn and remind me I haven't eaten in ten-plus hours. I make sure I'm on the right heading and march off.

As I head up a series of steep switchbacks, I pull out my last MRE meal. I eat as I trudge up the mountain. The route is a series of peaks and valleys with creeks and a river thrown in just for the heck of it.

If I'm lucky, the river will wash the stink off me.

Fourteen hours later it's dark when I curse at my soggy boots. They haven't dried out after the river crossing. I'm about to cross another country road when lights come on and a HUMVEE rolls to a stop next to me.

Master Sergeant Levitt gets out and tells me to hop in the back. When I don't move right away, he goes to his command voice. "It's an order, Wolf."

"Hooah, sergeant," I say walking around the back. I find it odd I'm the only one. I dump my rucksack and enjoy the immediate sensation of lightness. I sit on the floor behind the cab to stay out of the wind.

Now I realize I'm still wet. I shake from the breeze-induced hypothermia.

My mind flashes with images of my mother and bio father camping, foraging, and hunting on the reservation. I smile and I forget the cold for a minute.

Then the scene dissolves to a laughing Kingman. I shiver before anger fuels my body with the heat of revenge.

FIFTEEN

NORTH GEORGIA

There are two other candidates when we arrive at Camp Merrill. I'm told to check my gear, restock, and be ready to move out in the morning.

First thing I do is clean my weapon while eating two MREs. I eat everything but the wrappers. Then I repack my ruck and dump the dirt out of my load-bearing equipment. After everything else is done, I take a shower and attend to my cuts and scrapes.

I'm human again and set my alarm to wake up a 0430, a half hour before morning PT.

I hate being right, but I'm ready when we form up and take off for a run. Instructor Blain sets an eight-minute-per-mile pace, which isn't fast, but my knees and lower back complain.

Thirty-five minutes later, I fall into a rhythm. The pain amps up on the way back as we do sprints at the seven-minute-a-mile standard.

Blain stays out front, and I let him. I'm just making sure I'm faster than the other two guys. When we return, I'm just behind Blain, who is breathing a lot harder than I am.

"Grab chow and report to the classroom at 0700," he huffed.

We report, and the other two guys are told to wait in the barracks. Inside the plywood paneled room is a six-foot-long table with four instructors sitting behind it and two more off to my right. I come to attention.

"At ease, Wolf," Captain Carpenter said. "I want to commend you on your long walk. No one has ever covered so much distance before."

"Thank you, sir."

"But being a beast and knowing how to navigate are just table stakes here at the RRC. We need smart soldiers who can think on their feet. Men who can pick up and apply new technologies and stay undetected for days and weeks at a time. Are you one of those soldiers, Wolf?"

"Yes, sir."

"We'll see."

The next three hours and forty minutes is the most intense non-combat time of my brief career. I answer questions on everything from basic Army tasks to coming up with an ad hoc plan to surveil a target.

I'm buried under an avalanche of questions. There are esoteric weapons specifications and lifesaving procedures.

It ends with me briefing back an operations order for a four-man team to surveil the Plant Vogtle nuclear power station southeast of Augusta.

I sigh when I walk outdoors after being released. The inquisition left me feeling drained. When I reach the barracks, I find one of the RRC team members and a bunch of radio gear.

I'm taught the Digital Message Device Group, DMDG; it has a computer like keyboard and replaces a morse code key paddle.

I pick it up and spend the rest of the day learning antennas and setting them up. I'm not sure why antenna theory makes sense, but it does.

When we are all back in the barracks, they give us coordinates, time hacks and fifteen minutes to prepare. Before we leave, we are each assigned a radio and DMDG to carry in addition to what we already have. We repack our rucks, then head out.

We spend most of the next two days on our feet moving through the mountains. We hit our marks and communicate the key items we find during surveillance. On the third morning we are handed peer reviews.

We fill out the reviews, and the instructor orders us into the back of his pickup. Back at Camp Merrill again, they tell us to clean up and report to the classroom.

I'm the first to enter and find a sour-looking crowd of frowns and shaking heads. Master Sergeant Levitt starts in. "Damn, Wolf, we had high hopes."

Blain points a knife hand at me. "And I thought…"

In my tired and less than optimal operating state, I'm prepping myself for the letdown, and it must be showing on my face. Levitt and the rest of the instructors laugh at my expense.

"Welcome to the RRC, Wolf!" Captain Carpenter said.

I can't help myself. I'm smiling ear to ear and chuckling.

"Now the real training starts. Based on the needs of your team you will go to HALO, advanced mission planning, sniper, and camera courses. Then covert and clandestine tradecraft," the captain said.

I'm assigned to Team One. No new guy hazing like in Ranger Bat. It's all business and all professional all the time. The operational tempo is high. If we are not on actual missions, I am in training.

The next five years go by in a blink. I'm traveling all over the world, seeing places I've only read about in National Geographic. I love it. I keep in touch with Morgan, who is still working out of the embassy in Colombia.

I'm thinking about Special Forces again when we are a greenlighted for an actual mission in Panama of all places.

I know General Noriega is a narcissistic dictator, but I'm surprised to find out how deep he is in with the Colombian cartels. Instead of a runway or power-plant, Noriega's Panama City residence is our target.

CHAPTER
SIXTEEN

PANAMA CITY, PANAMA,
DECEMBER 16, 1989

We fly commercial air into Tocumen International outside Panama City. Two to a flight, all originating from different cites is the USA. Our cover stories include telecom engineers and documentary film crew.

We augment our basic set of cameras and recording devices with a pre-planned kit. It's delivered by an Army Intelligence and Security Command element at Howard Air Force Base. A signals intelligence specialist four describes one of the spectrum analysis devices as sensitive enough to pick up the static from a bird fart.

I appreciate his expertise, but he reminds me of Gollum from the Lord of the Rings books. Dude needs more time in the sun around real people.

Our target is northeast of downtown in a ritzy neighborhood, Altos del Golf. The estate sits in the woods, and reports indicate substantial physical and electronic security. The house was built like a Y with the base as the entrance. Off to its right is a square box, which is the barracks for Noriega's security element.

At the top of the Y is a pad with a helicopter occupying the space. We suspect plenty of guns and heavy weapons in the house and barracks. Our indicator Noriega is in the residence is the roadblocks on the road to the northwest and southeast.

We will confirm he is onsite after we spike the house with our listening devices and cars with RF beacons.

Our intel says the compound and the house have the latest in physical and electronic security. When at the house, Noriega makes use of encrypted communications to talk with the cartels and his allies.

Between the money he gets from the drug cartels and his association with the Agency, we expect state-of-the-art systems.

Our friends at the Agency are being less than forthcoming with detailed information. There is BS about staff retirements, no records, blah blah blah. We don't need them.

Elevation is our response to the thick woods. In our pre-mission planning we identify a high-rise mixed-use building with offices and residences, to include rental units. The operations team rents us a unit facing our target on the sixteenth floor.

We install our equipment and begin around-the-clock electronic surveillance. Our mission is to fix his precise location.

As the sneakiest and most South American-looking member of our six-man team, I have the honor of the close-in work. As night falls, we sit around the table and war game my infill, actions on the objective, and exfil.

My primary method of infil and exfil is on foot. My alternate means is via whatever I can grab. If all hell breaks loose, the rest of the team will assault the nearest roadblock to create a diversion. Not intending to kill the Panamanian soldiers but to let me break contact.

If I'm discovered, I want my work to appear to be a burglary, not the activities of an intelligence agency.

At 0200 I take one last scan of the blueprints and cinch up my pack. Inside are two remote cameras, four listening devices, a PVS-7-night vision binocular, and a Nikon camera.

Before I head downstairs, I amble into the bedroom I share with a teammate and close the door. I sit on the floor and meditate, then sing my death song. My parents and my spirit guide join me. I'm at peace when I stand.

As I leave our building, I avoid any kind of direct or indirect lighting. The trees provide the concealment I need to access the adjacent park. I pass between the roadblocks.

The security teams are focused outward. I approach from the west side of the house and sprint from one grove of trees across the road to another.

When I arrive at the other side I slide onto my belly. I slip my arms out of my backpack and adjust it so I can access my tech.

To make it hard for Panamanian direction-finding teams, we encrypt our radio communications and configure narrow band antennas. Inside the encryption we have created code words and phrases for additional operational security.

A NASA Space Shuttle mission is overhead, and we use their lingo.

"STS main, STS Three-Three," I say radioing our command post.

"Shuttle Three-Three, go."

"I pass California," I say indicating I've arrived at the west wall of the house.

"Roger that, Three-Three."

I strap my night vision headgear on. I hate the awkward headband setup but cinch it down and scan for people. Not seeing any, I flip it up and go for my tech.

First up, I scan for passive infrared motion detectors and beam barriers.

There are detectors at the corners of the house, but they don't overlap. Then I check if they are dual band IR and Doppler radar devices. I'm not finding anything in the frequency bands of those sensors. I grab my bag and scurry to the dead zone.

Two feet above my head are three thin slot windows, for lack of a better description. The windows are angled out. I still my breathing and lower my heart rate. I should be outside of Noriega's office. I pull a listening device from my pack, turn it on, and extend the antenna.

I use a telescopic antenna to stick it to the top of window frame, where it's out of sight. Multiple people enter the room.

I lower myself to the ground. My Spanish is a lot better since Colombia. Angry questions then a "Yes, El Jefe" concerning a late drug delivery. Another voice answers the phone.

"It's for you, General."

Jackpot! It's him.

CHAPTER
SEVENTEEN
ALTOS DEL GOLF ESTATES

Three men, from the voices, in the room. Grumbling I can't make out, feet shuffling, and then a door closes. I wait for another five minutes and decide whoever is in the room has left. I scamper back to the trees.

"STS main, STS Three-Three," I say.

"Shuttle Three-Three, go."

"I have Kennedy audio," I say, confirming the target.

"Roger that, Three-Three. Charlie Mike."

Our master sergeant clears me to continue the mission. Clockwise around the property and house makes sense versus tripping what should be more alarms near the front of the house.

Detectors out, I scan the left side of the Y and observe a concentration of passive IR at the corner. RF too, but it all ends a few feet inside the tree line. I sling my pack and give it another ten feet just in case.

The blueprints indicate a bedroom at the end of the spur. Its windows are sliding glass doors. The lights are off, and the only noise at this side of the house is the hum of the air conditioner.

I continue my clockwise movement and check the next wall intersection seeing the same overlapping IR and RF motion sensors.

The dead spot must be due to poor or no maintenance.

I give the next corner a plenty of space then slip into the middle of the Y. My kid self wants this to be like hide and seek on steroids. The problem here is getting caught won't be funny. I take a step and freeze.

A cigarette.

I didn't sense whoever it is, but he or she is close. I focus on as little movement as possible. My mind is screaming! Don't shift your feet. Don't stare.

There's a sigh and crackling. I smell the acrid smoke from the steam. Then footsteps heading away from me into the center of the Y.

I flip my night vision down, and there are people milling about.

I need to close the distance to count how many.

As I stalk my way forward, I scan the house for entry points and anything not on our six-year-old blueprints. On this side, the wall appears to be solid concrete with brick overlay at regular intervals.

The drawing of the house indicates it's fortified. It's going on 0300 when I arrive at the base of the Y. It surprises me to find four armed men on a large patio, they're whispering.

Their whisperings seem tense and choppy, off in a weird way. A couple of naked women step outside the multi-pane sliders and beg for the guys to come inside. The men laugh, and two break off and follow the women.

There's no chance of entry here so, I work my way to the edge of the trees. It's another hundred feet of open space to the other side of the Y. The open area leads to the helicopter pad.

If I head north the gap is less than thirty feet, the best option.

As I head toward the smaller gap, I don't spot anyone watching the helicopter. I continue and scan the space around it and confirm no guard. I want to steal it, take it for a joy ride but I don't know how to fly one.

Can I cripple it?

"STS main, STS Three-Three," I radio.

"Shuttle Three-Three, go."

"I want to adjust this unit's fuel air ratio, over," I say knowing they can see me with the night vision camera.

"Stand by Three-Three."

As they're researching my question I hide on the far side of the bird and raise on my toes to find the hatch. I've seen Huey and Black Hawk crews fuel, so finding the first of the two gas caps isn't hard.

I'm removing the gas cap when my radio breaks.

"Shuttle Three-Three, STS main, the ratio can be adjusted with the organic supplement stored under the floor. Copy over."

"Roger, copy out," I say and smile. I back off the concrete pad and use my knife to cut the turf up. Underneath is just what I want, sandy dirt. I grab a handful and in it goes.

I go back and grab another before laying the turf down. I skinny under the helicopter and come up on the house side.

I open the panel and undo the cap. It slips from my hand, clanging against the skin.

I spin on the cap and close the access panel. I roll under the helicopter and glance back to the house. Men with flashlights are coming. I sprint back to the trees and move left, to a thicker grove.

This time instead of laying down, I climb. The weeping willow is full and offers concealment. I stay near the trunk, on the far side away from the guards, so I don't shake the limbs.

It's the same trick squirrels use. Man, they are mad. Could be my bias at play, but these guys and their boss are not use to working hard at all.

They spend another six minutes grumbling and messing about to make it seem like they are doing a thorough search, then head back.

I wait until they are back at the patio before I drop from the tree and reverse my course. The security team, or at least a few of them, are awake now. Time to pull back and let them settle down.

I have an hour and a half of darkness. I burrow between a thick bunch of trees and wait.

"Shuttle Three-Three, STS Main.

I pull my pack over my face to block the sound of my whispering. "Three-Three, go."

"RTB, out."

CHAPTER
EIGHTEEN
ALTOS DEL GOLF ESTATES

"Negative STS Actual, Charlie Mike," I say, trying to keep my voice neutral.

"Shuttle Three-Three. Return To Base."

What the heck is going on? I could have completed the mission, but now I'll have to go back, and that's bad. More trips into a target equals a higher chance I'll get discovered.

Being a team player has its pluses and minuses. I smirk thinking what Morgan would do. Just the opposite, of course.

But I'm a rule follower, most of the time. I move to the road and lower my night vision, noticing the dull headache I have from the barbaric head strap.

I see a cigarette hanging out a vehicle window to my right and there are two guards on the blacktop staring down the road. I sprint from grove to grove.

On the other side, I don't wait and slow to a fast walk to clear the area. Before I enter our building, I take off my night vision, turn off my radio, and stow it all in my pack. Now I'm just a weird guy who enjoys running at night.

I make time to unwind by taking the stairs to our floor. It's not helping. My mind is swirling with questions.

My past with my biological father comes into play, and I wonder what I've done wrong.

Two more flights of stairs, and it hits me. As a kid at six years old, my dad would show me how to do a thing one time and expect me to get it and do it perfectly from then on.

Of course, I couldn't, but it didn't stop him from being disappointed in his only son and calling me stupid. Why is this coming up now?

Ever since joining the Army I've set my path and goals. So far, I've completed everything I set out to do. As my mom used to say, it's your father's stuff to deal with, not yours. I put that thought front of mind.

The doors to the stairs are not one-way crash bars. I stop and listen before opening the door to our floor. I hear the faint sound of music and nothing else. We are two doors to the left of the stairs, and I enter our apartment unseen.

I drop my pack near the front door and stride into our ops center. Master Sergeant Bowen is arguing with a guy in civilian clothes.

"You idiots need to stick to surveillance. You could have tipped Noriega off that we are tracking him."

"But we haven't," Bowen said.

The man scowls at me. "Stay on mission," he said then spun and departed.

After the door closes, Bowen turns to me and sighs. "He was an embassy puke from Defense Intelligence Agency who showed up while you were onsite. He went ballistic when we watched you messing with the helicopter. I held him off for as long as I could before he ordered me to tell you to RTB."

"You know I could have completed my tasks, right?"

"Yeah, of course. You're the sneakiest warrior we've got," he said inside a chuckle. "Get some sleep."

"Roger that, I say unsure I can when my spirit guide tells me we'll be at war with Panama in twenty-four to forty-eight hours.

CHAPTER
NINETEEN
ALTOS DEL GOLF ESTATES

It's 0800 when I take my shift in our operations center. The log shows Noriega's staff arriving, picture-taking, and an exchange of guards.

I'm watching a middle-aged guy in a flight suit wearing Ray-Ban aviator sunglasses approach the helicopter. I swing the long-lens video camera to the helicopter pad.

My teammate Mikael Sandeberg, we call him Mike, wanders over with a cup of coffee. "Anything interesting?"

"Not yet, but soon. Check out the monitor."

"Nice! The dirt and sand should have settled to the bottom of the tank and its fuel pickup," he said and chuckled.

The pilot does his walkaround and jumps in the left seat. I grin at the sound of the turbine spooling up in the distance. The blades start to spin. There is a sputter, and the turbine whines to a stop.

The pilot hops out, opens the passenger door and disappears for a minute. He backs out with a shop towel in one hand and a stick in the other. After opening the fuel cap, he drops the stick in and pulls it out.

I zoom the camera in on his face and find furrowed brows and a clenched jaw. He walks around the front of the helicopter to the other tank and repeats the process.

This time, he bangs the stick against the strut, then drops it before walking toward the house.

"It's going to take a mechanic most of the day to clean it out, if not longer," Mike said, slapping my back.

"Great! He'll be using the SUVs I didn't get to tag," I say, shaking my head at last night's interruption.

"It's not a big deal, Wolf. The Joint Strike Team knows how to stay out of sight when tailing a target. Plus, it will set a pattern they can use to their advantage when whatever we are here for kicks off."

"It kicks off tonight," Bowen said from behind us.

I spin in my chair. "Did you get a time?"

"JST at 0130. The main force at 0200."

"Who they sending?" Mike asked.

"Ranger regiment, 82nd, 7th Infantry Division and more. Full-on invasion of Panama."

"Do we go hot or stay covert?" I ask.

"Hot. Our H-hour mission is to contain Noriega to this location if he stays the night."

"Do I need to change my visit from setting the beacons to disabling the SUVs?"

Bowen stared out the window to the target. "Yes, makes sense. But priority one is putting more listening devices on the house and security barracks."

"What about power?" Mike asked.

"Our friends at the National Security Agency will take care of that."

"This is shaping up to be a busy night at a sub-optimal time," Mike said.

I laugh. "Come on, brother. Is there ever an optimal time for what we do?" I say and glance back at the video camera.

Four armed guards stand back from the helicopter as the pilot tries to start it up again. The entire process takes a little less time than the first try but ends with the same result.

The pilot jumps out hands palms up, pointing to the engine. The security guys come closer and gesture. The pilot flips off the helicopter, walks away with the guards trailing.

"Nice work, Wolf," Bowen said.

Mike and I talk for a few minutes more about what we'll take tonight and how we'll split up the tech. Then he leaves to pack.

Seven minutes later the door to Noriega's office opens and he's barking mad that the helicopter isn't working. He's expecting a twelve-minute flight, but now he's facing a thirty-five to forty-minute drive to his office at Fort Amador.

He rants for another minute and other voices promise to get the helicopter fixed as soon as possible.

Noriega screams for the idiots to get out, then makes a call. It might be about money and accounts, maybe banks, but he's using a lot of code. He hangs up and leaves, slamming the door.

I turn and make sure it's all recorded. I burst the message out over the satellite link to NSA.

Seventeen minutes later, I watch the general board an SUV and log its departure. It's picked up by the road guards who sandwich the president front and rear. As they drive off, I'm left with my thoughts.

Six years after experiencing my first combat I'm about to take part in another invasion. But this time I'm working for the JST on the priority one target. And once again, there is a drug connection.

I haven't lost my hatred for the cartels, heck, the whole drug supply chain. The thought reignites my desire to get down south and fight them where they live.

But first I need to focus on the fight in front of me. All kidding aside, Mike is right. Tonight's mission is not optimal. And if we get discovered or caught it can blow the JST snatch of General Noriega.

It's not hide and seek. It's combat, and I will be carrying a full load of ammo, carbine, pistol, and explosives.

Tonight is life or death.

ALTOS DEL GOLF ESTATES, DECEMBER 19, 1989

Mike and I will leave at 2030 to gather any last-minute intel we can give to the assaulters before they do their thing.

Mike takes his time studying the blueprints and overhead pictures. "I'll take the extension, and you can work the house. It will put you closer to the guard barracks."

"I like it. According to the drawings, half of the building is another armory, there are lots of opportunities for the taking," I say and laugh.

Mike shook his tilted head and suppressed a smile. "Don't get caught up in the opportunities and forget the primary mission."

I smile. "Roger that," I say, knowing he knows me too well. We will finish our initial mission on the west side of the compound. Then, we are assigned the blocking, early warning position on the road leading to the house.

There's bound to be a weapon or two we can use in the armory against the Panamanian Defense Force as they race to protect Noriega, and I plan to borrow it.

We brief our plan to Bowen and after his approval, coordinate with the rest of the team. Coordination complete, we check our packs and tactical kit one more time before taking a break. Mike lets me have the bedroom to meditate and sing my death song.

I put on my pack and jump twice to ensure I'm as quiet as possible. I glance at Mike, and he nods. I sling my rifle and put my pack on over the sling, so it rides tight to my side. My untucked shirt covers my pistol belt.

We're now on the west side of the house. After a dozen minutes of listening and watching, we've identified a guard who roves from the front door to the side of the house and looks north.

There's also a guard roving from the extension to the side of the house and looking south.

We take a knee facing opposite directions. I pull Mike close and whisper. "Their pattern has changed. They didn't do this last night."

"Roger that. I count six minutes between visits for the sentry where I'm headed."

"Mine is a four-minute interval."

"Lucky you," he said, his bright white teeth glowing in my gray-green world.

"Yeah, lucky me. See you at the road crossing," I say and thump Mike's thigh.

After he disappears, I scuttle through the gap to the side of the house. Sneaking between the bushes and the side of the house, I still my body and lower my heart rate to listen.

When I don't hear anything, I lower my pack and withdraw a listening device, power it up, and attach it to my probe, which I extend. Nothing. I stand off to the side and place the device on the window frame, then lower myself back down.

I retrace my path back to the trees on the north side of the guard barracks. It's 2348, and I settle in waiting for the assault.

It's time. I sprint to the shadows under a barracks window. I can sense helicopters before I hear them and this time it's no different. I turn on my infrared beacon and hope I don't get lit up by a trigger-happy crew chief.

Four little bird helicopters fly over as two MH-60's hold position over the trees.

There's yelling coming from inside, then a helicopter lets loose with a mini gun at the door leading to the barracks. I use the distraction to sneak back around to the parking area door and enter the building. I take a knee at a door on my right to get below the potential line of fire.

The firefight grows to a howl then becomes intermittent. I'm surprised no one is running for a vehicle or to flank the helicopters overhead. I throw the door open, expecting return fire. Nothing. I close the door behind me and break out into a grin.

Just what I'm hoping for. There are racks of M-16s, AKs, and RPGs. I grab a backpack of rockets and an RPG launcher then open the door and clear the hallway. I exit the barracks and haul the mail to the trees. "One-four, One-six approach imminent," I radio.

"Roger that, One-six."

I drop to the ground next to Mike and whisper. "Brought firepower if they show up with armor," I say, sliding the RGP between us.

He smiles ear to ear, his head bobbing like a mad man.

"Do you hear anything?" I ask.

"What?"

"Exactly. It's quiet, no shooting or gun runs."

"STS Three-Three, STS Main. Dry hole. I say again, dry hole. Switch to channel four."

I let Mike respond for us. "Roger that. Switching to channel four."

"I don't get the dry hole. We have voice recordings of him after the motorcade returned earlier today," I say.

Mike holds his hands up. "Who knows? Let's go find out."

Just then the sky lights up with tracers, and I listen to the howl of the miniguns. It's followed by the repeating boom, boom, boom, boom of 40mm twin cannon round impacts. An AC-130 is over the city delivering hell on earth. The invasion of Panama is on.

Our earpieces come alive. "STS, Black Knight Actual. Meet us in the driveway. We need help with intel collection. Copy?

We respond and walk out to the road. I radio. "Black Night Actual, STS two in the road, IR beacons on."

"Copy, we see you. Cleared to advance."

I remind myself to breathe. I hate entering a position filled with amped-up shooters. When we get to the house, Sergeant Major Meeks, a legend in the Ranger community meets us and leads us to Noriega's office.

"We've gone through the documents but need your help with the PC and recording devices."

"Roger that," I say dropping my pack and sitting down in front of an IBM PS/2. I try several combinations of passwords and get locked out. I reboot the system. On the second try, I get access using his wife's name, Felicidad, and the year 1989.

I find a directory with a Lotus 1-2-3 spreadsheet labeled *suppliers*. I open it up and can't believe what I see. It has names, addresses and phone numbers of people in Panama, Colombia, Peru, and Chile.

I glance over to Mike who is playing with a tape recorder. He hits the play button, and it's Noriega's voice on speakers around the office.

"This is how he tricked us," Mike said. "What have you got?"

I stare at the keyboard and lie. "Nothing yet. I'll keep looking," I say. I force myself to breathe. I feel tingly all over. This can't be real.

"I'm going to check the other rooms where we placed the listening devices," Mike said.

I check to my left, and I turn the dot matrix printer on. I enter the print command and stride to the door and close it. While it prints, I scan the room for the container of the floppy disks.

I find them in a desk drawer and put them in my pack.

When the print job completes, I delete the file and the directory, and reformat the drive sector. I stuff the printout in my pack, then I shut down the PC.

I disconnect the monitor and stack the tape player on the PC. I open the door in time to see Bowen.

"What am I going to do with you, Wolf?" he asked. "What you got?"

"Mission accomplished, master sergeant," I say, trying not to grin.

"One tape recorder with high-quality recordings of Noriega's voice and a PC full of solid intel. Mike is looking for more."

There is movement at the door, and I raise my rifle over Bowen's shoulder as he spins.

"Easy trooper, same side," a guy in L.L. Bean tropical outfit said. "Who are you guys? You're not with Meeks."

"Depends on who you are," Bowen said, pushing my barrel down.

"My name is Ward Jensen, and I'm with the Agency. I'll be leaving with the PC," he said, showing his credentials and stepping toward me.

I raise my rifle. "I don't think so. This is a military operation, and you can have it when we get done."

"Master Sergeant Bowen, can you tell your dog to back off and stick to the reservation where he belongs?"

The darkness came from deep within me. I punch my barrel into his gut, drop my rifle and land all five knuckles on his bent-over chin. He drops like a sack of potatoes. I stand over him and yell a war cry before I realize Bowen has me in a bear hug.

He lifts me off my feet and growls. "Enough, Wolf. You're done here," he said as he lets me go. "Get back to the command post and help the rest of the team pack."

I will the fire to simmer down. "Sorry, boss," I say and walk out.

CHAPTER
TWENTY-ONE

ALTOS DEL GOLF ESTATES,
DECEMBER 19, 1989

On the way back, I see flashes of light from bombs and hear their thunder. There are red and green tracers racing through the sky. I make sure I'm not seen.

I don't want to be a target for the Panamanians or our guys. When I get to the relative safety of the building I stop at the stairs and sit on the steps.

I've just let my desire to hurt the drug cartels, and anyone involved in the trade crush my integrity. I don't lie, but I just have. Have I started on the path to become like them, dishonest and self-serving?

I can't let it happen. Do I turn myself or the data in? What if I don't? Can I, with Morgan's help target the names on the list?

Is it tainted because of how I acquired it? Am I tainted?

My thoughts are a mess. The only way I know to slow them down is to get physical. I sprint up the stairs. I'm on the ninth floor, and all I can focus on is my breathing. When I get to our floor, I'm met in the hallway by Remi. "Dude, we felt you pounding up the stairs, what gives?"

"I just messed up. Not sure how much longer I'll be here."

"We got word. Bowen says to keep an eye on you. You seem okay to me. Are you operational?"

"Yeah, I'm tight. I'm here to do my penitence and help pack."

"Outstanding. Come on, we're getting lifted out from the roof in seventy-five minutes."

Remi's arm around my shoulder feels like forgiveness, and it's cool coming from a teammate.

But it's not his forgiveness I need.

It's mine.

The short helicopter ride to Howard Air Force Base provides a perspective of the fight still going on around Panama City. La Comandancia, the Panamanian military headquarters, is all torn up, and what's left is burning.

The AC-130 did serious damage. There are troops in contact and tracers light up the sky, but none are come our way.

Bowen hasn't uttered a word since returning from Noriega's house. Mike is tight-lipped but winks when I see him. There aren't any of the usual smiles and back slapping at having completed another successful reconnaissance mission.

When we get to Howard, a C-130 is waiting for the six of us. We cross load, strap our gear down and take off in twelve minutes. It's an hour and ten minutes after we take off when Bowen sits down next to me. I take my foam earplugs out and nod.

"A real jerk move on Jensen's part, Wolf. But you can't go off like that again. Regardless of what he said, next time it will end your career."

"I get it... I need to let it go. It's just words."

"That's not all. He claims you or Mike have floppy disks from the office. He threatened to have the FBI arrest us and search our houses and barracks for classified material," he said staring into my eyes. "I know you guys wouldn't take sensitive materials and not report it, so

I told him go ahead. I expect the feds to be waiting when we get back."

"Let them investigate; there's nothing to find. I think Noriega destroyed them and tried to wipe the computer before leaving," I say.

"Roger that. Command holds us to a higher standard."

"I appreciate you having my back. It will not happen again," I say while focusing on making sure I keep the promise.

Bowen calls the guys together and we walk through a hot wash of the mission yelling over the sound of the four-engine beast.

Now I'm seeing the team relax and have a bit of fun. When Bowen asks me to relay the Agency story. I get a bunch of "Good for you" responses.

"Tighten up, knuckle draggers. Dropping idiots from partner agencies is not the fast path to glory or a long career," Bowen said. "He threatened cavity inspections when we land."

Only I know the floppies are secure in the Top Secret Sensitive Compartmented Information and cryptographic materials portable safe Remi guards with his life. Ninety-nine percent of the FBI employees and about zero of the field agents have the clearance to access the case.

Our standard operating procedure clears Remi to use deadly force to defend it until it's opened inside our SCIF —back at Fort Lewis.

I have access; they don't. Thanks for the tutorial, Morgan. As for the printout, it's inside a space in my backpack where it would take complete disassembly of the pack to find.

I could use the information to embarrass the Agency and maybe get Jensen fired. But that's not my goal. I want to get it to Morgan and put the names on the list out of business. I can't do that while continuing to work for the RRC. I love these guys like brothers, but ...

It's decision time. Do I try for a slot behind the fence with the JST, or head to Special Forces selection? What's the quickest way into the counter-drug fight?

Nine hours later, we land. At our company and team

cages, there's no FBI. I breathe a little easier. We head to the arms room and clean our weapons.

We check them in and meet up with the rest of the guys in our team room for the full after-action report. The company commander joins us and commends us for a job well done.

We go home and life goes on.

The following weekend I head to the Seattle airport and the DHL office. I place my sealed package with the list in one of their Express Worldwide envelopes.

Then I pay cash to ship the package to the address of the safe house where I spent the night with Danny.

Phase one of my plan is in play.

CHAPTER
TWENTY-TWO

FORT BRAGG NORTH CAROLINA, MARCH 16, 1990

It takes ten weeks to get a slot for Special Forces assessment. While I'm waiting, I get news I'm on the promotion list to E-6 Staff Sergeant. It's a nice bump in pay.

When I get to Fort Bragg it's right back to basics and proving I belong. The Special Forces Assessment and Selection course is twenty-one days of finding out who has prepared physically and is mentally ready for the next phase of training.

They teach the newbies and non-infantry soldiers everything they need to know before assessing their capabilities to perform under stress. Thirty percent self-select out during the first several days of physical grinder.

The second week in, I help where I can. Eight guys haven't patrolled since basic training and they plus another six are weak when it comes to land navigation.

We do everything with fifty-five pounds in our rucksacks. Run, march, run and march at night, all night. Hurt backs, twisted ankles, lost during the compass course. More men are dropped from the course.

During the third week we are in teams, and the instructors rotate the student leaders. They task us to carry and or push heavy loads for long distances.

Assessment becomes a series of personal tests, within team tests and several get recycled. One classic example is a hot head seemly well-prepared guy who gets frustrated right in front of the cadre and declares that he will do the team task himself. He doesn't get team. He's pulled aside and we don't see him again.

A former 2nd Ranger Battalion instructor watches my every move, order I give, and critiques my leadership style. I roger up and point out I am, and we are, always on target on time.

When I devise a unique way to pull a heavy load like a draft horse team, an instructor finds out and takes away our wheels to see what I'll do. After he leaves, triumphant smirk on his face we bend the poles to make a sled—hey no one said we couldn't—we make it to the target on time.

Because of our team, the cadre makes more rules, and future teams won't have it as easy as we did.

I'm the top student of my class, and it seems like cheating, but I'll take it. No stupid marching tests. I should get my wish list choices.

Seventh Special Forces Group and 18D medic. When my orders come down, I get one of two, 7th Group. The story I'm told is, there aren't any medic slots available right now, instead they assign me 18B weapons.

I want medic, but waiting for the slot and the training will add up to another eighteen months before I get into the fight. At least weapons at six months gets me into the fight faster.

The course is known as one of the easier special forces military occupational specialties. But it's packed full of data about light weapons like pistols, rifles, and machine guns.

I'm taught their characteristics, how to assemble, disassemble, diagnose, and correct problems. I'm surprised by the number of written tests followed by hands-on tests with time limits.

The recent change, we are told, is not to make us gunsmiths but experts at combat deployment of the weapons.

I spend extra hours at the school with one instructor named Todd talking about suppressors. From simple makeshift aka expedient one-time use versions to units, which reduce the sound signature to the mechanical operation of the weapon.

One pistol system to catch my eye is called the Hush Puppy. It's a Navy invention. It locks the slide of a Smith and Wesson semi-auto pistol making it silent. I also learn it's not just the can, as the suppressors are called, but the powder load keeping the bullet subsonic.

I'm not sure I'll ever need this James Bond type of weaponry, but it's nice to know it exists in the Army inventory.

We lose a few people at different spots in the hands-on training. One of them is my roommate, Larry, who is great when there's no stress. He's recycled and I've got my room by myself for the rest of the course.

I'm one of the few volunteers to take a light weapons test blindfolded. As a visual guy I see the pistol or rifle in my mind's eye as complete units I can take apart and return to functional.

I'm not the fastest--dropping an AK bolt on the floor doesn't help, but it is a fun challenge.

It's not all fun and guns, though. We still work out every morning and study like school kids at night. The 18B "schoolhouse" is right next to a building called a vertical wind tunnel. It sounds like a C-130 when they are training high-altitude low-opening free-fall students.

During lunch once or twice a week I head over there and talk shop with the instructors. I want to go to the course before I get assigned to my team.

I'm trained on anti-tank weapons including Russian, Chinese, and NATO versions that can kill a battle tank. Then the instructors switch to air defense systems called Man-Portable Air Defense MANPADs.

There's a video-game-like simulator, where I get to shoot down helicopters and low-flying aircraft... cool.

The training turns harder for me when we switch to heavy weapons, aka mortars and their deployment via a Fire Direction Center. There's a bit of sorcery in the setup of a mortar team, with poles and sights on the mortar tubes.

But I get two other solid teammates and we get into a rhythm.

The instructors encourage competition. We start with the 60mm mortar and finish with the gigantic 120mm beast. My favorite is the 81mm mortar.

We need to know it all so we can train partner-country armies like the Ecuadorians, Colombians, and Peruvians where I'm headed in South America.

At the end, of course, the final application of all we've learned is in a firebase scenario. There are defensive positions to man, call for fire missions and at the very end a mad minute, during which we are alternate high-explosive rounds and illumination rounds out of 60mm and 81mm mortars.

After the late night we are told to report at 0900. I can't sleep. I get the shower hot and spend a long time working the kinks out then blink my eyes open in front of the mirror.

At the schoolhouse we spend the day cleaning weapons, getting our grades and orders to other schools. Most guys get their team assignments.

Todd hands me mine and chuckles. "You should get into politics, Wolf. You got a slot at free fall school. How'd you, do it?"

"My dashing good looks and witty banter?"

He grimaces and shakes his head.

"Okay, maybe it's finding the one instructor who is interested in Native American warrior culture and offering to take him to the reservation to experience it firsthand."

"That I'll believe. How do I get on the list?"

"You just did, brother," I say and high five Todd.

The first week of the military free fall course includes a quick introduction and then right into the wind tunnel. It reminds me of putting an arm out the window of a car, like when you're going sixty plus, and you surf your hand up and down.

I think my wrestling background helps, as I have awareness of where my hands and feet are relative to the rest of my body. I pick up on the idea I'm diverting air as I move my feet and hands.

I'm no savant. It takes a couple of flights in the tunnel, but then it moves from being a challenge to pure joy. I dream of flying.

The instructors are all top-notch and solid guys. They call me blackbird, which is fitting.

Learning to pack the parachutes is nerve-racking, as we jump the parachutes we pack—under supervision, of course. I take consolation in the fact our back-up parachutes are packed by professionals called riggers. There's all the names of the pieces and parts plus the cables, which must be routed just right.

We hang in our harnesses and practice emergency procedures. Like we did in jump school, but this time "Another One Bites the Dust" is not screaming out of the loudspeakers. In basic airborne school we have one handle to protect and pull.

Now it's two ripcords, one for the main parachute and one for the backup, called the reserve. There's also a thing called a pillow you pull to release your parachute if it's a mess.

It's all new and coming fast. Once again, we join up in groups and study after the day is done. During this first phase we are also taught/introduced to the full spectrum of military free fall operations.

A couple of my stepfather's friends made HALO jumps into Vietnam, Laos, Cambodia and even North Vietnam. Their harnesses and parachutes are nothing like this new gear based on advancements from the skydiving community.

The next three weeks is jumping from C-130s at altitudes starting at ten thousand feet and increasing to twenty-five thousand feet. We start off with what are called Hollywood jumps.

We are not carrying any equipment like rucksacks or weapons, and on our first three, two instructors follow us out. As we demonstrate proficiency, it drops to one instructor. After my first jump, I'm assigned one instructor, named Jake.

We are now jumping day and night with gear, all of them at altitudes requiring oxygen. It's my twenty-first jump. I'm all kitted up for combat with night vision googles, my rifle, chest rig, body armor, and a Carl Gustaf recoilless rifle tube across my waist.

It's cold at eighteen-thousand feet above ground flying at one hundred and thirty miles per hour.

Tonight, I'm the last student in the stick for this pass and feeling pumped by my advancement. I'm even thinking about taking up skydiving; this flying my body thing is addictive.

I stand up with the stick, check my gear and the student in front of me. Then I spin to have Jake check mine. He studies me and nods. I give him a thumbs-up and focus on relaxed breathing.

The jump light turns from red to green, and the stick moves forward with the instructors leaving the ramp. Jake and I jump, and once I stabilize, I find him in my night vision and get a thumbs-up.

I spin left, then right. I track for a three count and flare, check the surrounding space then wave off and pull my ripcord.

Nothing happens. I check over my shoulder, tilting my body, which should get clean air to the pilot chute. Still nothing. I check my altimeter, and I'm going through twenty-five hundred feet.

Prior to every jump they have briefed us. Twenty-five hundred feet is the lower limit they permit us to fall without a parachute. I can't see the malfunction.

I pull the left ripcord and black out as the reserve parachute snaps open with enough g-force to slosh my brain around in its housing. I wake up to the radio squawking in my ear. It's Jake yelling at me to wake up.

I shake my head to clear the cobwebs and reach up to grab the steering loops. This canopy is smaller than the primary parachute. I get my bearings, head into the wind and put my feet together.

I flare the canopy late and twist, impacting feet, knee, butt and back. It's sloppy but I'm in one piece and laughing the kind of laugh following a holy crap moment.

I see Jake land next to me. He kneels. "You okay, Wolf?"

"I think so. I'll find out for sure when I stand up."

"Okay, let's get you up," he says, dropping his rig.

He turns on his headlamp, and the white light blinds me for a second. I shield my eyes and hold out a hand. I release my ruck and struggle to my feet.

Here's the problem. In the dark I didn't see it even though it's just three inches off my waist.

"Jake check this out," I say, pointing to where the pilot chute line is wrapped around the barrel of the Carl Gustaf tube I have strapped across my waist.

"You're six up versus six down. Doesn't matter how ugly it is, that's a positive ending to the story."

"Thanks to my spirit guide," I say, rolling up the reserve. I hoist my ruck, and we head to the pickup point.

The rest of the course is anti-climactic. As the honor student I get to kneel on the ramp with Jake during our end-of-course "fun jump" and watch as he corrects the aircraft heading. It's a

Hollywood jump, and we exit right after another student and instructor.

Jake and I fly down to them and position ourselves four feet away.

I'm under a clean canopy at three thousand feet and play with spiraling down. At one point I have the sensation of going backwards, and then let go of the steering loop. I find the wind line and stand up on my thirtieth jump.

It's been a blast, but I'm ready to join a team and head south.

CHAPTER
TWENTY-FOUR

FORT BRAGG, NOVEMBER 27, 1990

I've just gotten back from leave skydiving in Florida and find my assignment to an Operational Detachment Alpha ODA and orders to report to 7th Group are missing.

Operation Desert Shield has kicked off in support of our Kuwaiti coalition partner. Most special forces personnel, especially those lacking combat experience, are trying to get assigned or attached to 5th Group—the group supporting the commander of US Central Command, General Schwarzkopf.

I'm not interested. My focus is one hundred percent on getting back to Colombia. I'm at U.S. Army Special Operations Command bothering the administration division to straighten this out.

"It happens, sergeant. You're one of the lucky fifty a month whose orders get dropped out of seven hundred and thirty-two thousand soldiers of the United States Army. We'll assign you a position number and cut the orders. But it will take a few days. Check back on Friday," Private 1st Class Tilly says, scanning a printout.

"I appreciate the help," I say, using the mess to lock in my assignment to Morgan's team. "I'm already assigned to ODA 7210. They are expecting me. Can we make sure we don't introduce more problems by keeping the team assignment the same?"

"Sure, I got you covered, Sergeant Wolf. Check back Friday," she said again, shooing me out of the office.

"Before I go, is there anything I can do in appreciation for your helping me, PFC Tilly?"

My mom taught me when asking for a favor, I should ask what I can do for the other person. Andy says it's the best way to make connections and friends in the Army.

He told me to make friends in finance, so I'll always get paid, in supply and at the chow hall, and if no one else, the admin types, as they can help or mess up your career.

And to be honest, I feel good when I help another person.

Tilly's eyes are wide, and her mouth hangs open for a beat. Then she composes herself. Her eyes twinkle and her cheeks flush. She stands and scans over her cubical wall to see if anyone is listening, then leans forward.

She whispers. "My name is Anna. I'll think of something. See you Friday."

I nod, spin, and walk away. I've got butterflies in my stomach and I'm smiling. I think she took my honest ask as flirting, and I guess it might have come across as such.

Later in the day, I'm at a loss to explain the position I'm in. From my early days in the Army, when my every thought, facial expression, and status of my uniform and equipment was analyzed and graded to floating in the no-man's-land of the training pipeline. It's creeping me out, like a weird episode of "The Twilight Zone."

My first thought is to get more jumps, but the free fall course can't use a newbie. The Green Beret skydiving club only jumps on the weekends and holidays.

A sergeant first class from the club chuckles as he tells me to enjoy the best of Fayetteville, the city next to Fort Bragg.

Fifteen years after the official end of the Vietnam War it's still known as Fayettenam. A seedy collection of bars, used car dealers, tattoo shops, Army surplus stores, and "gentlemen's clubs."

It's not my cup of tea, as the saying goes. I beg Todd at the weapons committee to let me help until I get my orders.

"You can hang, but you can't teach unless you've gone through the instructor course. Although I can have you assist during the hands-on exercises. You good with that?"

"Yeah, it's this or go stir crazy," I say.

The rest of the week goes by in a flash as I assist during the light weapons phase. When I'm not helping students, I dive into briefings the committee gets from vendors and the Defense Advanced Research Projects Agency.

It's the first time I've heard of the agency, and the more I get to know about all they do, the spookier it gets.

On the weapons side they are looking at materials to make our rifles lighter and more lethal. They are designing plastic cased cartridges that hold three projectiles.

In the sci-fi category, they are developing directed energy weapons, the key issue being power. The handheld portion of the weapon is small by comparison. The power source needs a two-ton truck to haul it around.

The rest of the week is a blur, just as I like it. Doing versus sitting around. When Tilly's office opens at 0800. I'm first at the door and stride to Tilly's cubicle. She smiles and nods as I return the smile and sit in the chair beside her desk.

"Your orders are in the printer run this morning. They should be ready for pickup by lunch time today."

"Thank you," I say and lean closer to her. "Did you consider my offer?"

"I want to go to a Garth Brooks concert," she says and drops her head, sighing through her frown. "But the closest location is Dallas."

Well, played I think as I suppress a smile. "When do my orders say I have to report?"

"This coming Wednesday."

I've been set up, but I like it. "Okay, it means we need to leave tonight out of Raleigh. I'll head over to Moral, Welfare, and Recreation MWR to get airline, hotel, and concert tickets. Do you have a car?"

"Yes," she says and grins.

"Can you get off after the print run?"

"I think so."

Her smile and excitement are infectious. I've never done anything this spur of moment before. "Okay, pick me up at fourteen hundred, and I'll get us a seventeen hundred flight to Dallas."

I suppress my wanting to squeeze her hand. I stand feeling electricity between us. Money's not a problem; I put half of my pay into savings every month.

It feels like I've given myself permission to let go. I've never spent this kind of money on a weekend or with a woman before.

I admit I don't really understand women other than my mom, in her mom role. Anna is different. If nothing else, this weekend with her in Dallas will be fun.

CHAPTER
TWENTY-FIVE
DALLAS TEXAS, DECEMBER 1, 1990

After the concert at the state fairgrounds, we are out till 0200 laughing and having fun closing a honky-tonk bar. There's tension, and an altercation when one patron doesn't like us as a couple.

He's spewing racial slurs at me when Anna steps up and lets him know we are active military. She pointed to me. "He's a combat vet. They call him Wolf for a reason. You don't want to find out."

He calls bull crap and throws Anna aside to get to me. I step inside his wild swing and block and deliver a punch to his diaphragm. I cringe as he spews his stinking hot breath my way.

The heel of my hand finds his jaw, and there's a crunching sound as my ankle trip sends him crashing down.

I'm back in my defensive posture and glimpse one of the bartenders on the phone. I motion to Anna, and we sit in an empty booth and wait for the police.

Another bartender brings us a couple of waters. "I saw what happened. You defended yourself."

"Thanks. I'm Wolf, this is Anna."

"You look like you're Blackfoot or Crow," he says.

"Crow and you? Querechos or Comanche?" I ask, using the old name for Apache.

"Comanche. David Tosahwi."

"Lance Bear Wolf, good to meet you."

While we wait for the police, David and I trade growing up on the reservation stories that have Anna laughing and shaking her head at our antics.

It takes five minutes to tell the police our version of the story, which is backed up by David. They check our IDs and tell us the incident will be written up but not to worry.

The other guys will get the citations. They tell us to be safe as they let us go.

"You are more romantic than you let on, Lance Bear Wolf."

It's my turn to smile as the blood flows into my face and neck. Breakfast in bed is one of those things I saw Andy do for my mom, and her appreciation at the gesture is what stuck with me.

We've got the room until noon Monday. We eat, drink coffee then shower together. We are in bed for a couple more hours until we venture out from the Marriott.

I'm interested in the book depository and area around the John F Kennedy assassination. Anna agrees to walk to Dealey Plaza.

Along the way we stop and chat about how the United States has changed since November 22, 1963.

We head east to Pacific Park, where we sit on the grass and talk about the Army and our futures. I tell her about my love for the history and cultures of the natives from Canada to the tip of South America.

She gets my wanting to join 7th Group and the draw of southern hemisphere. I leave out hunting drug cartels and describe Andy as my biological father.

Anna confides in me she's waiting for an Officer Candidate School OCS opening. She has most of her bachelor's degree completed. She wants to become a psychological operations officer.

I joke with her that setting me up for the concert and trip is an indication of how successful she will be. She punches my shoulder, and we laugh.

We head back to the hotel and don't go back out until late, just in time to get the last of the barbecue from a hole-in-the-wall joint the front desk attendant tells us about.

We are sitting outside their closed doors eating out of to-go containers when a man approaches asking us in Spanish if we have anything we can spare for his family. I see a woman and two kids looking on from the nearby corner and touch Anna's arm.

She nods, and I jump up and tell the man to hold on. I bang on the restaurant door until the man who is closing cracks it open.

"What do you want? We're closed," he said with a growl.

"Here's sixty bucks. Give me whatever you can. Doesn't matter what or how much."

"I can't," he said, shaking his head.

"Here's another forty. Please?" I ask, pushing the hundred dollars into his hands.

He stares at me. "I'll be right back."

Six minutes later he hands me two large bags. "You're a good man," he said, and locked the door.

"Please, tell your family to join us," Anna said, in Spanish.

For the next hour the world melts away as we learn about Jose, Carla and their two children, Luis and Sarita.

When they head for the mission where they will spend the night, I'm smiling inside. I've done a positive thing. Enriching life instead of taking it.

Anna puts her arm over my shoulders and squeezes. "You've got a big heart, Lance Bear Wolf. It's not what I've experienced in the macho world we live in. Your humility and heart will set you apart."

I smile and kiss her on the cheek. "Thanks. It all comes from my mom."

"She must be an amazing woman to raise a warrior who lives with compassion."

Anna wouldn't talk like this if she knew the darkness lurking in my heart.

On Wednesday, I'll reset and select violence as my default option.

"Hello. Who's calling?"

"Hey, Mom, it's me. How you guys doing?"

She covered the phone, and I heard a muffled voice. "Andy, it's Lance."

Andy picked up the other phone and Mom asked. "Son, good to hear your voice. What's the noise in the background? Where are you now?"

"The Miami airport, on the way to Colombia. There were a couple of small delays, but my 7th Group assignment came through."

"Good for you. It's not going to be dangerous like the *training* you went through, is it?"

"No, I'll be working out of the embassy in Bogota to start. There will be training missions, maybe even at the school I attended."

"Hey kid, congrats on the assignment. But I thought you'd want to be in the desert with the rest of the horde they're assembling," Andy said.

"Nah, if they need me, they'll tell me. I've got some—"

"Your mom's gone to refill her coffee. You can talk."

"I'm working an opportunity with a joint task force is all I can say over this open line."

"Roger that. When you get to Bogota, find a Marion MacKay. He's an old friend, works for the DEA. He got stationed there about fourteen months ago. Runs a program called SNOWCAP. Ah, thank you, dear. Coffee refill."

"I appreciate it, Andy. I've been following the program."

"No chance you'll get back for the holidays this year?" Mom asked as I hear her come back on the line.

"Sorry, mom. I need to get myself established with the team and folks at the State Department."

"We understand," she said, a tinge of sadness seeping through.

I change the subject. "You never told me what's up with you guys."

"Not much, but we are looking into the idea of spending our winters farther south."

"Great idea! Winters on the reservation are brutal. Where?"

"Tucson. The houses are cheap, and it's a simple drive."

"You're right. I'll be able to fly into Phoenix and be there in less than two hours."

"I love the thought, Lance."

The announcement for my flight blared over the speakers.

"You've got to go, don't you?"

"Yeah, it's time to board the plane."

"Okay. Write or call when you can. And Lance, don't think for a minute I don't know what we are fighting in Colombia. Promise me you won't let the dark wolf rule your days, okay?"

"Will do. Love you. Bye," I say, staring at the handset before I place it back in the payphone cradle. I hope, I find a woman to share my life with who is as smart and insightful as my mom. I muse, is it Tilly after she completes officer candidate school.

Five hours later, I see Morgan. I'd learned the Army had promoted him to sergeant first class. I wonder how long it will be till he's demoted again.

After a handshake and back slap, he starts in. "How did you wrangle a spot on *my* team?" he asks, leading me outside to a black van.

I throw my bags in the back, and we sit on the bench behind the driver, who looks Colombian.

"It's okay to talk?"

"Yeah, Marti's cool. Right, Marti?"

"I hear nothing, Mister Morgan," Marti says, flashing a grin in the rearview mirror.

"A friend worked a deal with the detailer who is sweet on her. She got your senior weapons guy a slot at the intel course, which lets your junior guy move up, and I move in."

"Excellent, you're learning how to navigate the battlefield we know as Army career progression." he says and belly laughs.

"There is an art to it, isn't there?" I say, inside a chuckle.

"Agreed. And now you're in the big leagues. The ambassador controls everything going on in Colombia. It doesn't matter what agency or branch of service you are with.

Nothing happens without her knowledge and approval. It's frustrating most of the time and cool when one of my schemes works around all the controls she has put in place."

"How is her relationship with the DEA?"

"Rock solid. She's as anti-cartel as you and me."

"Excellent! Ever run into a guy named Marion MacKay?"

"How do you know the name?"

"My stepfather and he served together in Vietnam. I'm supposed to look him up."

"He spends most of his time in the field. I'll introduce you when he gets back," Morgan says, holding onto an overhead handle as we bob and weave through traffic.

We brush past a motorcyclist I could have touched outside my window. When I turned back, Morgan is sporting his signature wide-eyed politician-style smile.

"You know, Wolf, I think we're going to do some good."

TWENTY-SEVEN
MILITARY ATTACHÉ OFFICE, US EMBASSY, BOGOTA, COLOMBIA

"Who's our priority-one target?" I ask.

Morgan holds his hands out over the list I sent him. It's spread out on the table. "Everyone, but the reality is it depends. Who can we build a case against that gets us the resources we need to conduct an operation?"

"You make this sound like a law enforcement operation."

"It's exactly what it is, Wolf. We are not free to operate as we please. We can't just run around and end these guys, much less pick them up for interrogation without Colombian help."

Morgan taps his ear, then points to the ceiling.

"Understood. One of the special forces tenets is to work through the partner country to achieve outcomes positive for our partners and the United States," I say and nod.

"Let's check you in with DEA and see when your dad's friend gets back," Morgan said.

We take a wandering route to the DEA wing of the embassy. Built since my last visit, it holds three times more staff and several Colombian police and military officers. We walk past them to a small office where a tall, thin man sits behind a computer banging away like he's on a search and destroy mission.

"Henry," Morgan said. When the man doesn't look up, he turns his display sideways and sticks his smiling face in its place. The guy jumps like he's gotten an electrical shock.

"Jeez, Morgan, you scared me. Put it back."

"As you can see, Henry here has insane focus. He does more top-shelf work for the DEA than everyone else combined in Colombia."

I stick my hand out. "Lance Bear Wolf, new guy here. Good to meet you."

"You, too," Henry said, gripping my hand, his spindly fingers enclosing mine like crab legs. Such a strange feeling.

He lets go and repositions his display before standing. "If Morgan moves, you can stand in front of the wall, and I'll get your picture for a permanent badge."

Picture taken, Henry offers me a temporary badge and has me review and sign a non-disclosure agreement. "You're good to go, Wolf."

"Do you need my clearance or to read me on?" I ask wondering if my Department Of Defense clearance transfers without my needing to do more paperwork and watch the obligatory security videos.

"No. Your clearance is already in the system. A PFC Tilly forwarded it from Fort Bragg. Like the Army's special access programs, you will be provided access to the DEA equivalent when needed. The folks in the vault need help. We're glad you're here."

"Thanks, Henry," I say and follow Morgan through the mantrap double-door portal into the Secure Compartmented Information Facility, aka vault.

The door closes behind us and Morgan spins. "Here's the situation. Our team commander, Captain Gooden, is cool with us supporting DEA as it aligns with our quote training mission. We are tasked to train select military and police forces in basic infantry through advanced Ranger-like tactics."

"Cool, what's my role?" I ask.

"You and I will focus on the Cali cartel. The rest of the team works out of your favorite school at Tolemaida. The rub, so to speak, is the one-star general military attaché who wants us to stick to approved support only.

What he fails to see is the cartels are a national security issue just like the Revolutionary Armed Forces of Colombia. We call them FARC, like fart but with a k," Morgan said.

"Seems logical the FARC and drug lords are working together."

"Not yet, which is good. As of now, the communist guerrillas hate the cartels for subverting the purity of the future Colombia they are fighting for. The Medellin cartel is on the way out, the Colombian government is focused on Cali. Most of the people on the list work for the Cali cartel, which is a plus."

And so, the grind begins. The good news is I'm getting a master's class in intelligence collection and targeting. The bad news is how infrequent my field time becomes as I get branded the technical collection quasi-expert.

My familiarity with advanced communications systems and three-letter-agency gear translates to me being a technology nerd.

My clearance is bumped up to include DEA and NSA special programs. But not before I get a deep-cavity inspection, my term for interrogation, on my whole life including the bar fight in Dallas.

The lead intelligence officer at the embassy has me take a polygraph. I pass because I tell the truth.

Lucky for me, they only ask if I've ever stolen government property, and I can respond no, as what I stole belonged to Panama's dictator.

Clearance granted and passed to the DEA and the Agency, I dive in. I learn via on-the-job training. It's a mash-up of signals intel, bugs, and GPS-linked trackers.

Bogota, Colombia December 1992

"Morgan, I don't give a crap about the merit badges and framed certificates. I'm going stir crazy. I need to get into the field," I say, demanding a chance to work outside the embassy, go undercover.

"Sure. All you needed to do is ask," Morgan said.

I clench my fists and snort. "I've been busting my butt with all this high-speed, low-drag equipment for the last couple of years, and all I needed to do was ask?"

"Yeah, we thought you liked it, and you are the best at it, so—"

I close my eyes, shake my head, and vow to always ask for what I want.

"Got just the operation for you. DEA thinks it's a cartel issue we shouldn't get involved with, but I see it as path to putting you inside the cartel."

"What's that?"

"The idiots from FARC have kidnapped the daughter of Cali leader Jose Londono and are demanding a ransom of ten million in US dollars."

"Sounds like the DEA is right. It's not directly related to the drug war. Why do you think it's worth our time?" I ask.

"Simple. With your tech and our confidential informants, you can locate the daughter. Her name is Christina Santa Cruz London. You find her then lead the raid to get her back. You'll be an instant hero and deeper in the cartel than anyone has ever been before."

"Why me?"

"Because unlike the rest of us gringos you can go native, pilgrim."

"You know it never ends well for us natives in John Wayne movies, right?"

"Okay, I'll drop the reference. You're still the best choice for the job."

"I'll need a strong backstory and cover for why I'm able to find her location without spilling classified."

"The Agency will help with the backstory while you task the collection resources," Morgan said, and smiles.

Now he's got me smiling, too, darn it.

"Roger that. The FARC can run, but they can't hide."

TWENTY-EIGHT

US EMBASSY, BOGOTA, COLOMBIA, FEBRUARY 8, 1993

"She's here," I say, pointing to a circle I've made on a map of Bogota's Ciudad Bolivar slum. Twenty-seven days of tasking satellite and special mission aircraft assets to narrow down the search area to a quarter mile.

"Where did you say?" Morgan asked with a tilt of his head. "Sorry. I'm reading a request for training."

"Here, in the slums."

He scratches the stubble on his chin. "Does it seem strange to you the FARC would bring her to Bogota?"

"Yeah, but it's where the intel leads."

"If the cartel finds out, they'll go in hot and heavy. It'll be a massacre. We need to get the guerrillas to move her into the countryside."

"They don't know me. I can go in and snoop around. It will make them move her."

"Ha! Great idea, Einstein. It will also make you dead," Morgan said and huffed.

"I'll go in as an aid worker, ask questions, and bug out."

"Sketchy. The slums are owned by FARC, but it's made up of territories run by militant gangs who kill people for crossing into their turf. It's like Los Angeles and being a Crip who ends up on a Blood-controlled street. A fast path to dead."

"There has to be a humanitarian organization servicing the area."

"Yeah, there is one."

"Who has those contacts?"

"You ever hear of USAID, our international development agency?"

"Yep, but isn't it an Agency front?"

"I can neither confirm nor deny," Morgan said, laughing at the tired joke. "No, those folks do genuine work to improve the lives of Colombians and thousands of displaced natives and Venezuelans."

"Cool. Will they cooperate with us?"

"Maybe."

"What's that mean?"

"They can be a little touchy about military and law enforcement involvement. In the past they've seen both types abuse their relationship."

"I'll let you handle it, considering you are the best marketing and sales guy I know."

"Why you so mean?" Morgan said in a whiny voice as he leaves the SCIF.

I return to my tech, not giving a second thought to the slum and how operating there might be different. I'm focused on narrowing down the search area. I want to get close enough to cause concern for the kidnappers.

My watch says it's been over an hour. What's taking so long?

My terminal beeps, and there's another bundle of radio transmissions the signals intelligence satellite has picked up from the target area. There is one NSA at Fort Meade has decrypted. It reads like a call for help.

Need a doctor, hurry.

Is it for Christina, or someone else?

The door to the SCIF flies open, banging against the wall. Morgan strides in, his wide smile, looking like rows of Chiclets gum. "They're good with your drugs and violence survey. And I previewed our plan with the DEA ops lead, and he approves."

"A survey? Who am I working for?"

"A nonprofit out of Houston called Hast International. A friend is CEO."

"How long before this sketchy cover story crashes and burns?"

He scans the SCIF and leans in. "My friend Buck Wild will answer the calls. I gave USAID his direct number. He's a lieutenant with a local emergency response team. It's the same area code as Houston."

"How do I get credentials proving I'm working for Hast International?"

"I know a guy."

"Of course you do. Check this out," I say, handing him the transcript.

"Damn, we can't spin up. No one goes in there at night who isn't FARC." Morgan said. He flops down in a chair, his fingers drumming the table.

"Well, we have more time to meet with your guy. I just hope they haven't hurt Christina."

We study the map, such as it is. It's several layered and pieced-together pictures with crayon colors to mark target-area boundaries and planned routes for my infiltration of the area. I will lead the USAID workers into the primary target area and push on alone if needed.

After more study, I get a sense of the slum's tight confines. There are streets with hundreds of houses packed between them. It also looks clean, which seems a paradox, considering all I know about slums is from National Geographic stories highlighting India and Bangladesh.

Back at the house, Lana makes another savory, mouth-watering meal. After dinner, I join her in the kitchen as she cleans up. I ask her about the slum, and she shakes her head and wipes a tear from her cheek. She must know people there.

"They are called the disposables, Señor Wolf. The street children, criminals, drug users, prostitutes, and beggars. The wealthy of Colombia see them as undesirable and have created death squads who hunt them at night. Many have no home and live in the sewer," she says and crosses herself before continuing. "We are disposable until Señor Morgan brings us here."

"I'm so glad he did, Lana," I say, smiling. "How does the FARC maintain control? It appears the criminals operate in the better parts of Bogota and then return to the area at night."

"Yes, it's true. All the minor criminals head to the better parts of the city. They pay the FARC a tax. They have their people in certain areas, and they pay armed gangs of kids to watch the rest."

She wipes at more tears. "My oldest son... part of a gang. He died in a gunfight... by paramilitaries." she says, chest heaving, gasping for air.

I give her a minute to calm down. "Can you show me where the FARC are on a map?"

She spins to the sink, her whole body shaking. "No, they will find out. They will kill us."

I put a hand on her shoulder and turn her to face me. Her head is down. "We have a friend in trouble. The guerrillas have kidnapped her. All you have to do is point, and it's just you and me. No one else will know," I say, crouching down to look into her eyes. "Morgan saved you and your family. Now you can do the same for another person who needs help."

She shook her head north and south.

I ran to my backpack and brought the map to her. "Why is there a circle here?" she asks pointing.

"This is where I thought I should start," I say, not revealing any of the intel behind the circle.

Lana eyes me, her brows knitted, her jaw clenched. Then she points to a spot inside my search circle.

I memorize the location as she turns back to her work. "Thank you," I say.

As I head to my room, I visualize the raid and rescue with a helicopter, lifting Christina and me up and away on a rescue cable. It lasts for a minute before I realize I need to get my head in the game. Unlike my time with Team One, I will be solo with no quick reaction force if I mess up.

The next morning, Morgan and MacKay school me on the difference between my previous missions and this one.

No weapon, except for a small folding knife.

My only lifeline a radio that may or may not work in the congested environment.

And two other guys who have no training. They will be a combination of fearful, mad at being played, and very motivated to get the heck out of the area.

Call it going undercover or a deniable advanced force operation. Whatever... someone with more experience should handle it.

I've got to do this. Am I being cocky? Arrogant? Is it my logical progression to take on more and move on from team to singleton missions?

I'm not about to admit I'm scared, which I am, but will acknowledge leaving the USAID team behind does put me in extreme danger.

Time to put my visual memory to good use. I study the map late into the night. I visualize possible routes in and then the target area, from three-hundred and sixty degrees.

I close my eyes and fly the routes into the area and out like I'm a crow cruising just over rooftops.

I'm on my feet, moving around the house like a weirdo. Lucky for me, Morgan and the ladies have gone to a café to listen to live music.

When my focus wanders, I stop. I return to my room and sit back to a wall and sing my death song.

My spirit guide has an odd sense of humor and lets me know she'll do the best she can.

TWENTY-NINE
BOGOTA COLUMBIA, FEBRUARY 10, 1993

My insertion into the Ciudad Bolivar slum is not high-speed or low drag. The rickety truck is packed over the sides, front to back. Our driver is the skeptical one.

When we meet, he half rolls his eyes and sighs. All he talks about is the danger of bringing new people into the slums.

My USAID counterpart appears to be right out of an Ivy League university. Glenn Beede is full of the let's save the world bubbly optimism one has when heading out in the world for the first time. I feel old around him, having seen more of the dark side.

We sit three across in front of the tiny truck. Glenn doesn't believe taking a survey will make a difference, but he's happy it's not his people having to do the work.

We head to an area called El Mirador at the base of a steep hillside below a strip-mining area. The paved road is full of potholes. Maintenance is not a priority.

Twenty minutes pass as we drive through a stretch of block-built houses, which devolve into mudbrick and tin-roof huts. The steepness of the nearby hillside reminds me of climbing Mount Rainier. What desperation drives one to live on a hillside with no power, water, or sanitation above such a rich and beautiful city?

Glenn taps my shoulder, and I see a group of armed men who, oddly enough, seem happy we are driving their way.

"Community security," he said. "Hired them to help on my first trip into the area."

Maybe this kid is smarter than I give him credit for. But are they FARC? The truck stops and I get out, followed by Glenn. One guy moves to my left, his AK at the ready. Another guy questions Glenn and points at me. I play dumb and smile.

"This is Lance, you can trust him. He's one of America's disposables, a Crow Indian," he said.

The leader of the group tilts his head and squints in my direction. "You are disposable?"

"In America, the natives, Indians from many tribes, are disposables. We continue to fight for our rights. We are lucky. We do not have death squads, just drug cartels trying to poison and kill us," I say back in Spanish, priming the pump.

Bingo... his eyes flare wide for a beat, then he nods. "The cartels are killing this land and making the rich wealthier, while they abuse and attack the poor. We fight for change."

"I know what it's like to fight for your people to stop the oppression," I say, hand to heart.

He gives me a nod like men do when then meet another man they know. He spins and orders the group to grab the packages in the back of the truck.

Weapons slung around to their backs; they carry two packages in each hand. Glenn and I have one in each hand. The driver stays behind.

We enter a dense area where more people are packed into the five hundred meters between roads than I've ever seen in my life. We are taken into a house and leave out a side entrance into another house.

We start walking into and out of house after house. After the tenth house, I lose my sense of direction. I can't see the sky, and I'm not sure when I will again.

My watch says it's thirty-six minutes later. We enter a warehouse-like building. The adjustment to the new brightness takes a beat. I peer up and see skylights of a sort, opaque fiberglass panels.

There are sliding doors at one end big enough for a vehicle to enter, which is odd. Maybe there's a hidden alley I didn't see on the overheads.

They've hidden this place well. I bet if I looked at the pictures now, I would recognize the place has multiple fake roofs to make it appear to be a collection of houses.

I scan from my left to right as I slow my pace and take in the racks of medical, weapons, and food supplies. A young girl gets my attention and takes my packages.

As I watch her walk to a long table where the other packages are stacked, I see Glenn getting a warm reception. I'm ignored for the moment. I amble over within earshot of his discussion.

He's talking to a man wearing a uniform with two bright stars, the rank of brigadier general. What I hear changes everything. The general is asking Glenn when his shipment of C-4 will arrive.

So much for aid work, Glenn is with the Agency. Punked again, by Morgan.

"Lance, join us," Glenn said without turning around.

"General Mendoza, this is Lance. He thinks you have Christina Santa Cruz London hidden in this area."

Outed. Every nerve ending in my body is on fire, telling me to run. My mind races through my options and none end well. Screw it! They'll learn the hard way I can fight.

Mendoza belly laughs and puts a hand on my shoulder. "My friend, it would be glorious indeed. But no, we are not FARC. Did Glenn not tell you? We have broken away, as the leadership is permitting its lieutenants to what you Americans call it, ah… team with the cartels. Their ideology has changed to focus on the evils of our government and share in the profits of the drug trade."

My mouth open, shaking head, dumbstruck look garners pity from Glenn. "Our friends here understand the drug cartels are the root of most evil in Colombia. We supply them with what we can for their fight."

"But why kidnap her if you want a partnership?"

"The FARC leadership is delusional in thinking how much power they wield. It's a show of force," Glenn said.

"They often move through the sewers to safe houses and could have moved into this area to throw off any investigation," Mendoza said, scratching his chin.

"Do you have a map?" I ask.

The general hollers, and the young lady who took my packages comes running and hands the general a sheaf of papers.

He unfolds a crude map and points. "We are here."

"They are here," I say, looking at the scale and pointing. "Two hundred and forty meters from here."

Mendoza tells the girl to get me clothes and to send a man over. She leaves, and a minute later a guy appears who wrinkles my nose. I switch to mouth breathing, so I don't gag.

He's Pigpen from Charlie Brown personified. The girl returns with clothes matching his and broken old dirty tennis shoes.

"You can call him Joe," Mendoza said. "Change clothes, and he will take you to the area."

"Here's a burner," Glenn said, handing me a cheap cell phone. "It has one number. If you get into trouble, we will attempt to support you."

"What about collateral? If there's a gun fight innocent folks will get hurt," I say.

"Mister Lance. There are gunfights every day in the Ciudad Bolivar. The people know how to protect themselves. Do you?" Mendoza asked.

"I do. Can I get something bigger than this pocketknife?" I ask, holding it palm up.

"Take this," Mendoza said, handing me his customized Browning High-Power."

"Keep the thirteenth round for yourself, you don't want to be caught," Glenn said, eyes boring into me.

"Great. Thanks for the positive send-off."

I take a minute after changing to sing my death song again. Then I find dirt to rub in my hair and on my face and feet. I can't wear the shoes, they're too small.

Showered clean extremities with these nasty clothes on is a dead giveaway, and I'm trying hard not to get dead. I show Joe the map and point to the target.

"Let's go," I say, getting a nod in return.

My pace count says we've gone two hundred meters from the warehouse. Joe slides into a darkened entry and stops with me on his heels.

My eyes water as he leans in and whispers. "Security ahead on the left, I see the tip of an AK barrel, look."

I lean out just far enough to peek down the alley with my left eye. It takes a minute before I see the barrel in the clutter of everything else in this foreign landscape. I lean back in. "Outer perimeter. Is there any way to get closer?"

"Yeah. The sewer. There will be an exit into the safe house or nearby."

"I pointed to my bare feet."

"It's okay, I'll lead."

Barefoot in a sewer. This just keeps getting better. Logical Lance says call it a day. My dark side says I need to do this so I can get inside and tear down a cartel.

We move parallel to the sentries, and Joe enters a poor-looking factory. There are men heating and hand hammering what looks to be scrap steel into knives and cooking equipment.

He nods to a guy sitting along the side at a makeshift table and takes us to an area behind the workshop. There, in the floor, is an access shaft and more of the odor I'm learning to hate.

He grabs a flashlight from several in a notch on the wall and lights the way, descending one-handed. I follow and find it dry and dirty, but mostly clean of debris.

It's easy to tell he's spent time in the sewer as he walks with a purpose. If we get separated, I'll be in a bad way.

He stops at an intersection and points the light up. There is a subtle mark on the roof from where we've come. Great. Now he's let me in on the secret code, all I have to do is make sure I've got a flashlight if I have to bug out. Oh wait, I don't!

Another hundred meters and the gut check starts. The sewer is getting wetter and cluttered with refuse. Joe kicks away a syringe and needle combo.

The smell has me coughing. I pull my shirt up over my nose, and the dirt and sweat residue does a decent job of filtering out the odors.

We walk another fifty meters, and I'm trying not to focus on what is squishing between my toes. He takes a right; ahead in the tunnel is a slice of light. Joe lifts a finger to his lips, and I nod.

He makes sure the way is clear as we stop at the ladder. I point to myself and make a climbing gesture before testing the bottom rung of the wooden ladder.

I step up, then another, and another without making a sound until my head finds the heat of the metal plate over the shaft. Through a slit I see a low wall, but thirty degrees of view doesn't tell me much.

I lower my heart rate and listen. The seven minutes I wait seem like an eternity. Hearing nothing, I attempt to slide the panel back and find it easy due to its thinness.

Raising my head, I execute a three-hundred-and-sixty-degree scan. I don't hesitate and scurry to the side of the house thinking I should have checked for signs of dogs.

Joe will have seen me hop out of the shaft and will follow or not. Either way, I need to see if she's here.

Out of the corner of my eye, I catch Joe waving me back to the shaft. I smile, shake my head and hug the side of the house, drawing the pistol. The front of the house appears to be to my left and I move in a tactical crouch.

There is a young guy armed with a submachine gun lounging out front. He doesn't seem too alert, making me wonder.

Across the street I find the real threat in an SUV backed into the brush. There are two guys with their heads on a swivel. One is trying to hide the fact he's smoking but doing a poor job of it.

I spin to check behind me then keep to the wall looking for access at the back of the house.

There's a deck over my head, but at my level nothing I can use to make entry. There is a stout-looking drainpipe just around the corner. I secure the pistol and start climbing. As I get to where I can jump to the deck the sliding doors open.

I scramble to the edge of the roof and hold on to the gutter with everything I have. A man and a woman close the slider behind them and have a heated discussion about bringing a doctor to the house.

The man argues the physician was blindfolded and threatened; he won't be a problem. The woman says it's not the doctor she's worried about, it's the men who went to get him stopped at bar for a drink and to buy cocaine.

The man tells her to stop worrying. She calls him names and storms back inside.

Target verified. I decide to force their hand. I let go, pushing off with my feet and crash land on the guy. He's out, and I remember why I enjoy carrying pistols in holsters.

The blood on the sights is mine. I throw the slider open and charge inside. A guy goes from bystander to target when he reaches for an AK. Two shots, and he's down.

The woman screams, and I hear yelling and feet pounding. There's a bunch of targets headed my way. I scoop up the AK and drag the woman behind the island. She's fighting me.

"Be still, and you will live. I'm not here for you," I say just before the wrecking crew floods the kitchen with automatic weapons fire.

The sound is deafening. I wait until they run dry then stand and shoot, making them all dive for cover.

I bolt for the deck and drop the AK so I can control my drainpipe descent. I sprint to the front in time to see Christina being pushed into the SUV. Two more SUVs follow as they roar away.

Rounds zipping by my feet make me turn and fire at the gunman trying to reach around the corner from the deck. I shoot back, run and slide into the shaft, landing on my butt in the filth.

I scramble to my feet and run. Behind me I hear yelling and rounds ricochet in the tunnel. I use my hand to feel for and find the corner when I'm grabbed.

I push the pistol into a chest. "Follow me, Mister Lance," Joe said.

"Good to see you, Joe," I say, lowering the pistol while I wonder how badly I messed up.

CHAPTER
THIRTY-ONE

US EMBASSY, BOGOTA, COLOMBIA

Two days later it's clear at least a part of my idea worked. The DEA gets word Christina has been moved out of the city. Our intercepts come to the same conclusion.

The only problem is I seemed to have scared the FARC into calling a truce with the cartel, and they've returned Christina to her father.

All the danger and no way in. I kick a trash can and realize I'm being childish.

I head to the gym and pick on the heavy bag until I'm a tired, sweaty mess. Sauna and a shower change my mood.

Morgan and the new DEA agent in charge are cool and talk about next time. I like their thinking. Just move on to the next operation; keep collecting intel.

I join MacKay and a SNOWCAP team on a couple of missions, and it's good to get back into the field. We capture tons of cocaine and manufacturing precursors with the help from the units the rest of the team has been training.

I'm promoted to E-7 Sergeant First Class, and I'm back to enjoying what I do.

Unknown to me, news of my technological acumen has made it to Fort Bragg. A knucklehead at the special forces branch decides I'm just the unicorn they need to fill a Special Operations Command position at the National Security Agency.

I have two weeks to report. I'm leaving Bogota, Colombia, where the temps during the day are sixty-five. It's a permanent change of station to Fort Meade, Maryland, where there is snow and icy rain.

It's an internalized form of whining, which I don't do a lot. I've gotten used to the warm humid air and Danny when I'm not locked away in the SCIF. The drab cold of Maryland isn't appealing. But I know snow and cold. Heck, I'm a Montanan.

When I sign in at the NSA, I find out I'm in a billet, a military term for a position called a Fellowship. This means I will be working assignments and learning the breadth and depth of the military intelligence agencies.

The list includes NSA, the Defense Intelligence Agency DIA, the National Reconnaissance Office NRO, and the service units like US Army Intelligence and Security Command INSCOM.

The next morning, I try to run my unease away. Bundled up against the cold, my legs feel heavy. I'm pounding the streets, instead of gliding with my usual lightness.

Around the four-mile mark my brain fog clears enough for me to understand. I label it trepidation, fear, nervousness of not being smart enough for this position.

Now I've named it and I own it. I'll use it as motivation in combination with my discipline. My legs free up and I find my stride.

I smile, knowing as with every other challenge in my Army career, I'll give it my all.

At work inside the NSA, it's like old home week as I put faces to the various voices I've interacted with from Colombia. I begin the deep dive into signals intelligence and its subcomponents.

SIGINT, as we call it, is the interception of signals like I managed in Bogota.

The other element I learn about is electronic intelligence, which is all the other forms of communications like computer-to-computer or computer-to-weapons systems. I nerd out over my shiny new desktop, which has the Intel Pentium processor.

I'm also learning the Mosaic web browser and the rapidly growing space called the Internet, but it's on a different desktop in an unclassified area.

May 1993

I'm seconded, as the Brits say, to a team working collection on two countries I think of as partners with America. I've been so focused on "bad guys" it didn't dawn on me we spy on all countries, friends or not.

It's at different levels based on our alliances, like the one called the Five-Eyes. We share select Top Secret level information with the United Kingdom, Canada, Australia, and New Zealand.

With other partners, we share at the Secret level, and it's known as Secret Releasable.

The focus is on Israel and Lebanon. The president of the United States and the Joint Chiefs are interested in what appears to be a buildup of Israeli military forces near the Lebanon border.

It's eye-opening to watch the NSA put its ground, satellite, and mobile units to work. When combined with human aka spy intelligence from the Agency and DIA, we know well in advance Israel will kick off the attack on the twenty-fifth or twenty-sixth of July.

It's ten days later when the Israel and Lebanon war ends, and I'm posted to DIA. Once again, the might of the military intelligence agencies focus on a possibly dangerous issue. This time it's Russia.

The information DIA's assets are feeding points to a brewing crisis of leadership. On the twenty-first of September Boris Yeltsin suspends the Duma and scraps the constitution.

I'm working with an Army guy, Kieran Kennedy. Yeah, he's a member of the Kennedy family, and he's following in his senator uncle's steps in intelligence. He's super smart and joined to save money for college, preferring to pay for it himself, versus using the trust fund.

On October fourth, the army sends tanks that shell the Russian

White House. They arrest the survivors and grant them amnesty after the December adoption of the constitution of the Russian Federation.

1993 ends with new insight. Just because American news outlets aren't reporting it doesn't mean we aren't watching it. By my count there are at least sixteen ongoing civil wars and conflicts at the end of the year.

And it doesn't include all the smaller brush fires or the war on drugs.

My view of the world at large and the people in it is bordering on cynical. I hunt for humanity and find it in people who serve something greater than themselves.

After the holiday break skydiving in Florida, I've renewed my spirit. I'm jazzed for my next assignment, the National Reconnaissance Office.

Its existence was once classified and was only revealed last year.

The NRO is staffed by the Navy and Air Force. I'm told it comes from the two services being at the forefront of satellite technology since its infancy. I'm now working in Virginia, sixty miles from my apartment in Maryland.

The commute takes three to four hours each day. After a week of one-hundred-and-twenty-mile round trip commutes, I find an old cottage to rent. It's in a sleepy little town called Herndon.

Now my commute is thirty minutes each day. I spend the first two weeks reading and getting limited-value briefings. I'm waiting on my clearance update so I can be approved for the special access programs I will support.

The security office just has a couple of questions to finish my update. When I enter the gray-on-gray room, a man and woman are standing around a small gray metal table.

They immediately show me their credentials. I suppress a laugh at the thought of Detective Joe Friday from *Dragnet*. The guy, Jared Williams, is a thin and gaunt-looking Air Force major with the Office of Special Investigation.

Linda Marks is a captain. Army Regulation 600-9 would classify her as obese. After the credential check, I sit in a gray metal chair without being told to.

"How can I help you?" I ask.

Williams plays like he's taken aback. It could be part of a good cop, bad cop scenario. They sit across from me.

Williams leans forward. "Sergeant First Class Wolf, two things we need to clear up—"

"Do you know a Louis Kingman?" Marks asked in an accusatory tone.

Ah, she's predictable as the bad cop. It would be disconcerting if they switched roles.

"Yes, of course. He is the drug dealer who supplied my biological father the heroin he overdosed on," I say and smile. "What's the second question?"

They glance at each other, which indicates to me they have not gotten on the same page or rehearsed their actions.

"You threatened to kill him," she said and slams her fist into the table.

"I did. I was fourteen and angry at Kingman and my father. But as you can tell, I didn't kill him."

Marks flushes. It's interesting to watch her body tense before she shouts. "He died Saturday night. You've been hiding your plan to kill him since you joined the Army!"

I'm numb, the scenarios I'd created are unlocked and swirling around my mind. I suppress a curse. "What did you just say?" I ask.

"Don't play like you're shocked at the news, Wolf. You killed him!"

I sigh as a wave of relief surprises me. "No shit," I say inside a chuckle.

Williams jumps in. "This isn't a laughing matter, sergeant."

Time to amp it up. I jump to my feet. The metal chair clangs on the floor behind me. "For the record, I'm happy he's dead. But if you're going to deny me the clearance upgrade based on the utterances of a distraught fourteen-year-old, you go ahead. You already know I was in a SCIF from noon Saturday until noon Sunday. So, if you want to push your theory, I'll have the Inspector General and the SOCOM four-star, a combat buddy of mine, investigate your quote `investigation.'"

"Are you threatening us, Sergeant Wolf?" Williams asked.

"I don't make threats. I state facts," I say, and leave for lunch. Afterwards I keep reading what I'm permitted to see. At 1645, just before the end of the average joe's workday, I'm summoned to the security office and sign the paperwork and associated NDAs.

The focus area, Weapons of Mass Destruction WMD. The job, tracking precursors.

At home by myself, I hardly eat any of my takeout combination Lo Mein. I explore the hole where I'd kept my hatred. I still despise drug cartels, dealers, and users alike but it's not the same.

The light is slow to brighten. But eventually it does, and I realize I can use that energy to focus on the scariest subject I've ever researched. I start by reading up on the 1972 Biological Weapons Convention and the 1993 Chemical Weapons Convention.

While the Agency experts track the people, we track the precursor shipments and listen to communications.

This time it's the Agency in the lead with NSA and NRO in support. I'm learning all about the WMD Russia still has. They are supposedly destroying them. I'm briefed on the stockpiles of nation states who have not signed either convention, including Syria, Iraq, Iran, and others.

I'm granted an extension to the end of the year, but before I know it, my Fellowship is up. I get kudos for being the first NCO and making a difference. I'm awarded a Defense Meritorious Service Medal, and I've made a lot of new friends.

I understand the defense intelligence community much better. I appreciate the complexity of this world and all that goes into keeping America safe day after day. Too bad, I'll never be able to tell anyone about the work being done on their behalf.

CHAPTER
THIRTY-THREE

FEBRUARY 1995

"You're kidding, right?" I ask from my three-week vacation at the drop zone in Deland, Florida.

"No. Any school or base you want," the branch detailer said.

He's my career manager, so to speak, and I've never heard of anyone being given this choice.

And speaking of choices, I need to decide if I'm committed to stay an NCO or go to warrant officer training. I visualize the different paths and see both require me to get to the 18F special forces intelligence school first.

The detailer asks if I'm still on the line. I want to be a team sergeant, so the answer is an easy one. "Put me in the next 18F intelligence course, please," I say.

"Standby." A couple of minutes later, he comes back. "Okay, the course starts the third week in March. Your orders will have you TDY for training starting today, so you're not burning leave time. I'll make the school orders start a week before the class, so you have time to switch from your sky god long-hair hippy look back to soldier."

"You sky dive?"

"Yeah, just starting. I hear Deland is where all the East Coast sky gods hang out."

"Not true. I'm here," I say inside a chuckle. "But hey, thanks for all you do."

"No problem, Wolf. Blue skies, brother."

"Roger that!"

He's not all wrong. My hair is long and I'm in shorts, T-shirt, and barefoot.

I spend another week skydiving and meet guys from a National Guard 20th Group HALO team. They're squared away like the guys I worked with in Colombia.

I follow them out on four jumps and take pictures with my Olympus helmet-mounted cameras. I catch them in freefall, and it elevates me to hero status.

With two days before I need to report, I load up my jeep and head to Fort Bragg.

The intel course is fourteen weeks long with ten in the schoolhouse, where I learn a lot about tactical intelligence. During the last month we wander Washington, D.C., and the agencies I worked with.

We're at our first stop, NSA, when the class learns about my Fellowship. Many think I should be awarded the military occupation specialty based on the Fellowship alone. I explain the difference between national-level and tactical-level intel and why the course is important for me. I get a thankful nod from the instructors.

Reflecting on it now, the Fellowship is probably a recruiting tactic. But the NSA is mistaken in thinking I prefer the inside of a SCIF to the outside of the real world.

When we graduate, I'm top of my class and ready to join an Operational Detachment Alpha and spend a couple of years doing intel stuff before taking over as a team sergeant.

But from somewhere deep inside the intelligence community, I get volunteered for a special mission team. My sources tell me it comes from the Warlock. A mythical person who directs black deniable operations around the globe on behalf of the United States of America.

I'm told to roger up and that there will be exponential returns on the investment of time and skills. The team I'm about to join sounds a lot like an intelligence support unit, but it isn't.

It's a ten-person team. It's mostly specialists not warriors, and it reports through the SOCOM commander to the Agency. And what do you know, its focus is Weapons of Mass Destruction.

Funny, not funny how that works. Who the hell has been moving me around like a chess piece for this?

In a quiet moment of meditation, as I'm deconstructing my thoughts to enter a state of no mind, my spirit guide flashes in my mind's eye. "Drug labs, the Fellowship, NRO, WMD... she says speaking in my head. Then, my parents appear, and I snap to the present.

I realize how long it's been, and I'm embarrassed. I call my parents to check in, and my mom picks up where we left off last time I called during the Fellowship.

"I'm putting you on speaker. What's new, Lance?" Mom asked.

"Ah, let's see. I'm back at Bragg. I completed the eighteen-foxtrot course. Distinguished graduate. Since then, it's been more training, briefings, and area analysis."

"No marching test, kid?" Andy asked, and they both laugh.

I laugh with them. "Nope."

"Lance, don't know if Bjorn has told you yet, but he's completed 160th Aviation Regiment selection."

"Not yet. That's awesome, I'll reach out and congratulate him. How's Sierra doing?"

"She's pushing hard, like you and Bjorn. She just got her obstetric residency at San Francisco University Hospital," Mom said.

We talk for another half hour about life on the reservation and family. Before disconnecting, I mention I will be out of touch for a few months.

Mom and Andy tell me they'll talk with their spirit guides to support me with courage and strength. I can hear my mom's voice tremble as she tells me to be careful.

"I love you, Mom. Thanks for always being there for me," I say and hang up.

June 1995

I'm back in northern Virginia, but this time, I'm getting trained by specialists at the Defense Threat Reduction Agency. First briefing in and this craziness shakes me.

The United States and other nations have created some truly evil biologicals. I'm introduced to what we find in nature like smallpox, Anthrax, Plague, Tularemia, Ebola, and Marburg.

We watch film from Russia's secret testing area on Vozrozhdeniya Island in the middle of the Aral Sea. A team has brought in monkeys, which are chained to posts. Then the Army deploys Marburg via aerosol.

The scientists watch the monkeys for signs of infections. Then the monkeys are sedated and taken to a lab for further study. We learn several times poor protocols have killed people in the nearby towns.

As I learn more, I talk with the instructors about the Russians' lack of safety practices and what it can mean. It doesn't seem much better as my teammates, and I review asset reports from our other target countries, Iraq and Iran.

We learn how to detect, test, and protect ourselves. Just when I'm getting as comfortable as I can be, our instructors take us to a new level of hell on earth.

Synthetic bioweapons do not follow the laws of natural biology and can be deployed in innovative ways. They can have extended incubation periods.

The mood is somber as the instructor describes a biological called binary weapons, which are separated into two components we cannot detect. There are advances in gene-splicing and using recombinant DNA as a messenger.

A cold shiver flashes up my spine and I breathe deeply to center myself.

We fly back to Bragg and are driven to an isolated facility, where they separate us.

I meet our commander, a Lieutenant Colonel Neil Gates. It seems theatrical, but these deep-cover special access programs can be like this.

My heart is pounding against my ribs.

THIRTY-FOUR
JULY 1995

"Sergeant First Class Wolf, your reputation proceeds you," Gates said.

"Thank you, sir."

"Don't thank me. As of now it means nothing."

The colonel strides to the front of the room. "Take a seat, Wolf… It will take everything you are to execute this operation. Your mission is the destruction of a covert Russian bioweapons lab," he said and clicked a remote to display a map.

"It's here, at Gelin-Batan. Twenty-one kilometers from the Caspian Sea."

"Sir, it's close to a populated area. Can you zoom in, please?"

"We think it's part of their cover," he said, zooming in until the scale at the lower right indicates one inch equals a thousand meters.

It looks like what we call a slot canyon back on the reservation. The image looks pixilated in a weird way. "Can you zoom to an inch equals a hundred meters?" I ask, knowing the satellite imagery has fidelity to less than a meter.

When the zoom stopped, it took a beat like looking at a Salvador Dali painting. Once I got it, it made sense. "Why are we targeting a shipping container holding area?"

"We believe the Russians have hidden a covert bioweapons lab in the containers and in the canyon walls on either side," Gates said, staring at the map then backing away.

"They say there's an eighty percent chance there is an operational lab is under those containers. Their high level of confidence comes from two containers Langley tracked to the site. They came from the Institute for Biological Instruments Design."

"Not good. They made the reactors used to grow bad things during the cold war," I say, remembering my training. "It's not likely they are just disposing of the containers."

"Agreed. Your pre-mission training begins when we leave here. The agency vetted a Russian family you will live with for the next six months while we complete other preparations. You'll get more tech training and chances to jump from perfectly good airplanes at very high altitudes... You ready to get after it, son?"

I like Gates, straight to the point, no bull. Am I ready to get after it, yes. Do I have reservations, of course. I am already thinking of exfil as more like escape and evade, darn right. "Yes, sir. Let's do it."

Mid-November 1995

Leadership is spooked and the launch date is moved up. I'm at Vaziani Air Base south of Tbilisi, Georgia. I'm wearing US Air Force crew clothes as we offload Javelin rounds for the 82nd Airborne. They're training with the Georgian Army.

The C-17 appears to be a stock model. But the crew is Air Force Special Operations out of Florida. Our flight plan takes the C-17 over the southern tip of Russia on the Caspian Sea through Turkmenistan to Tashkent, Uzbekistan. As soon as the ramp closes, I strip down and don my high-altitude high-opening jump gear.

Everything I am carrying is Russian or available to their tier one Spetsnaz unit, Alpha, except for the laser designator I will use to destroy the lab, if I can confirm its existence.

Night has fallen when we take off. I secure my oxygen mask, which is being fed from the plane system. Seventeen minutes later I'm disconnecting my hose to the plane and switching on my jump bottle.

I sing my death song and stand. Drop altitude is twenty-three thousand feet. When we reach it, the crew chief decompresses the plane and opens the left side door. The hydraulic wind blast deflector extends, and she steps back.

I own the door and do my jumpmaster checks. It's just me, but it's a safety ritual worth the two minutes it takes to complete.

I prefer, like most of us do, to jump in calm weather. It's not what I get tonight. I'm counting on being between squall bands but know the winds are likely to be squirrelly in the mountainous terrain of my planned landing area.

I've offset it from the target by eight thousand meters.

Above me the light is red. When we reach the drop point the light turns green, I leap out sideways. I'm facing into the wind blast, hands out wide and feet extended, surfing the air. I count to three and pull the ripcord for my main parachute.

It opens on the aircraft heading, and I check my panel. I start my stopwatch and course correct based on my compass. Between the bands of clouds, I can see my landmarks, which are the minimal lights from Gelin-Batan and Maraga to its northwest.

Now at sixteen thousand feet I take off my oxygen mask and feel the air rushing by. The lights at my landmarks are getting wider apart, and it means I'm flying much faster toward my landing area than planned.

I turn my parachute into the wind and have the feeling of being dragged backwards. Not good. The wind speed is much higher than the forward speed of my parachute.

I spiral down to lose altitude and see if the winds are lower. I check at fourteen then ten thousand feet above ground level and find a slight change. It's not enough.

Spiraling down will cause me to be further out than planned, but the extra patrolling is better than overshooting.

I pull down my night vision googles before I enter the cloud layer. I alternate holding down the left then the right toggle. At three thousand feet I'm racing above the trees. Landing this way will end the mission, and me, before it starts.

I rack my brain for options knowing landing in the trees is a must do, but likely painful. I've got four hundred military and skydiving jumps under my belt, and this is the craziest thing I've ever done.

The reserve parachute is smaller, so I'll have more forward speed, especially with the extra weight I'm carrying. I've seen what I'm about to do and the jumper landed okay.

A quick altimeter check shows I'm at two thousand feet. I turn into the wind and deploy my reserve chute without jettisoning my primary chute. Having two parachutes out at the same time makes for a great picture if you are not flying backwards even faster than before.

I grab the left side riser of the main canopy and pull the cutaway pillow. The chute tries to fly away, except for my death grip. I circle my left leg around the lines then let go to steer the reserve while continuing to fly backwards towards the trees.

I can tell I've slowed, but not enough. As I get down to one hundred and fifty feet, I release the toggles and steer with the front risers pulling down hard. I'm in an almost vertical drop when a gust picks me up like a wave, and the parachute falls behind me.

Time slows down. I'm in free fall. My parachute is useless behind and below me.

When the main chute catches in the trees, it pulls me farther out in front of the reserve. I tuck my arms in front of my face and squeeze my legs together preparing for a violent arrival.

When the cracking tree limbs and flying debris stop, all I hear is the wind, rain, and my groaning. My world is black. I'm upside down.

The pulsing in my head is the tell. I seem to be stretched tight between the main chute wrapped around my left foot and my rucksack below me.

Pre-mission, we completed a terrain analysis, but I failed to really study the trees. To my advantage the ones I've crashed into are very dense without the large rib cracking limbs of the trees back on the reservation.

I self-assess. I'm not hurt badly or leaking. I crunch myself up and slice away the main parachute lines. I take a breath and crunch again, cutting the last of the line.

I fall headfirst as I get my non-knife hand out in front of me. It feels like five or six feet onto hard pan.

CHAPTER
THIRTY-FIVE
GELIN-BATAN, RUSSIA

I reach to my helmet only to find my night vision goggles are gone. Stripped off in the trees, I guess. On my left side I feel for my rifle and its night vision scope. I remove my jump gear, wiping away a pound or two of tree needles and twigs.

I use my rifle scope to search for and find the parachutes. It takes more effort than I expect to rip them out of the trees.

I throw my pack on and head out. When I've got sky, I send my code via a Russian radio, *Itchikaate*, Crow for I'm good and continuing mission. Nine seconds later, a three-letter ACK confirms they received my transmission.

Time is my current enemy. Two hours and seventeen minutes later I'm standing in a tree and can see the lights I saw during the jump. Down at its base, I decide on a compass heading, one taking me to the southern end of Gelin-Batan and the target.

Three hours of climbs and descents remind me of RRC selection, and there are thirty-five minutes to nautical sunrise. I find a spot behind an old broken and weathered tree.

This is as far as I go today. I estimate I'm at fourteen hundred meters, which is outside the effective range of the laser designator. As the sun rises, I consume the landscape before me.

I think, not bad for rucking in the dark. Now I have a clear view of the target area, I'm at twelve hundred meters.

I've got to get closer to designate the target. But first I've got to identify key personnel. The primary confirmation is a scientist code named Hades. His real name, Alexander Borodin.

According to the file we have on him, the KGB enticed him to work on vaccines. Then he joined the dark side and began creating weapons that can wipe out the world's population.

The information they fed me indicates Borodin is driven from his home on the Caspian Sea to the lab Monday through Friday. Sometimes on Saturday.

It being Tuesday, I have three to four days to identify him and his car, an AvtoVAZ 2110 sedan. But by stopping where I have, I've lost time I'll need to move closer to ensure I can execute the identification and then prosecute the target.

An hour later I'm seeing a pattern develop for the outer perimeter patrols. After noon, a jeep-like vehicle stops, and I watch a Russian soldier talk on a radio. He gets out and turns away.

His teammates stand and scan the valley then the mountainside. It's weird. They don't seem alarmed, like they're looking for me.

A sniper? The leader is gesturing and looks at the radio handset.

Is there a surveillance team or sniper nearby, or is it an electronic barrier?

The primary reason I've never been compromised or apprehended during a reconnaissance mission is I move much slower than my teammates. The way the Russians patrol it appears I have freedom of movement until three hundred meters from the road.

If they have night vision, it will take more time. More time in which the Russians can find me and compromise the operation.

As the sun goes down, I eat a ration and drink from my bladder. When it's dark, I sing my death song and take off my boots, putting them in my ruck.

I'll patrol five hundred meters to the south to be sure. I make it to the road and put on my boots. Barefoot prints would raise an alarm.

There are lights to my left, and I bury myself in the scrub seventy-five meters from the dirt track.

A truck pulls up, and eighteen minutes later a sniper appears. The light from his night vision goggles makes him appear to be a green-eyed monster with a Dragunov sniper rifle.

His replacement stumbles up the mountain. He must be new to night vision. Feeling safe for the minute, I turn to my objective. It will take most of the night to reach it.

The ground is rising again as I explore the well-worn old soul of this rip in Mother Earth's surface. I find a crack in the rock where a spring stream spills over the cliff face.

It's two plus feet wide with boulders providing cover to my rear. I pull out my bivy sack and squeeze into the crack.

On my elbows, I have excellent line of sight to guard post. I know it's there because the guy inside popped a hand into view to flick his cigarette.

The coming sunrise will be the test. The cliff face will see direct sunlight for two to three hours. My camouflage must be perfect. I set up my hide and crawl in on my belly. It's cold, but I'll manage.

I roll on my side and burst out *ookkumme*, the Crow word for over-look and means I'm continuing the mission.

It's 0630 when workers start appearing. Then two sedans approach the guard post, and the guard takes a half step. He leans out enough to hold and scan the presented badges, front and back. He hands them back, and the sedan enters the tunnel. He waved the follow-up vehicle through.

I lower my binoculars and close my eyes. I visualize the four badges. One is Borodin's. I'm sure he's in the right rear seat.

It's 0842 and I have one data point. Hades is onsite. Good news. On the way out I should see a glimpse of him at the very least. If I do, it's confirmation to designate the target at his next appearance.

At 1528 the sedan rolls through the guard post. Borodin is visible as he spins to knock the ash from his pipe. He taps away while I match his image against the one in my head. It's him alright.

I send *bilee isee*, Crow for hell. Now it's up to the Warlock, he or she will order the B-2 bombers on their way.

During planning, my identification of Hades made sense. The designator requirement, not so much. With GPS and the targeting systems on the B-2's, I asked why I needed to illuminate the target.

Turns out the warheads are older Soviet tech smuggled out of Iran. I eat another ration and relieve myself in the bag. I let myself fall into my one-eye-open rest state.

I jerk awake. Did I fall asleep? Maybe. It's 0400. I down four packs of instant coffee and drink from my bladder. I grimace and stifle a cough.

The sunrise is beautiful and in stark contrast to the version of hell we are about to inflict on this solitary location.

Borodin shows up an hour early. I burst out *alaxawíichiwee*, Crow for judge, and peek at my watch. When I receive the ACK, a cold shiver courses along my spine.

I set up the mini tripod and turn on the laser to illuminate the target. In comes another ACK. I scan to make sure I'm not being watched and take down my netting before I grab my rifle and run in a combat crouch for a thicket.

The security team's proclivity to focus out and away from a site they are protecting is an advantage I'll take.

I scamper across the first dirt track as the warheads strike in rippling thunder. I can't help but stare for a beat. I turn back in time to watch the sniper I avoided stand up and gawk.

He's got his hand on his throat mic as I shoot him twice in the chest.

I run as fast as I can towards his location. When I kneel next to him, I strip off his throat mic and hold it to mine. A voice is yelling on the radio, and I choke out "intruder at cliff edge" in my far from perfect Russian.

I drop the mic, drag him back into his hide and haul butt for the trees. Yelling behind me turns to zips and splintering trees.

I throw myself to the forest floor and crawl. The odor of wounded pines fills the air. When I don't sense anymore hornets of death buzzing around me, I stand up and run.

It's twelve kilometers to my primary pickup.

The air changes around me. It's an Mi-8 transport and an Mi-24 flying tank for support.

My knees lift a little higher, and my ruck is lighter at the sight of the hunters.

The helicopters circle away, and I stop to catch my breath and take off my boots. I'll leave less of a trail barefoot. I drink from my backup canteen.

My water bladder is empty. I'm up and head west for Tinit, which is two ridgelines and a valley away.

With the helicopters circling, I'll have to stay in the woods. It will add to the distance and time necessary to make my primary pickup.

I stop and turn on the radio. I hold the antenna in one hand and the Digital Message Device in the other as I start running again. I have to slow to a fast walk.

I can't type the message and keep the antenna pointed in the right direction while running through the forest.

I focus on the message and wait until a semi-clear space and burst the message *iiluupe*, Crow for second, meaning I'm headed to the alternate pickup site in Chulat. It's ten kilometers to the south.

Three kilometers later they know I know. And they're mad. At the edge of town, I search for a clothesline full of men's clothes. There are plenty of clothes, but it must be ladies' day. I'm staying on the edge of town hunting for anything motorized.

The pulsing grows as the air fills with the sounds of helicopters from all directions. I need to head east and south to my escape and evasion corridor. There's a dam at a place called Vodokhranilishche.

At its southern end, where the river feeds the reservoir is where I need to be. I stop in a thicket and burst a message, *duarche*, Crow for moving camp and code for contingency pickup location.

I hope this works as I've burned through my primary and alternate landing zones. I only have one more after this. If they are blown it will be *make it up* time.

I cross an east/west paved road and sprint into the trees surrounding another farmhouse. I can hear the helicopters.

Have the Russians brought in more sophisticated gear and picked up on my transmission? Did they catch me crossing the road?

There's an old army jeep-like vehicle and a truck. It's twelve more kilometers to the reservoir. I've got to take one of these vehicles. I run for the jeep and hope I can start it.

I speak better Russian than I read it. I jump into the vehicle, fumble for a minute, then it starts, and I take off down a dirt road in front of me. On the horizon, the helicopters are circling. I've got a ten-minute max head start, which they can erase in five.

If anyone is watching, they're sure to think I'm crazy. I sing my death song out loud and ask my spirit guide for its wisdom one more time.

Now I'm climbing a series of switchbacks to crest a ridge and see the Mi-8 and Mi-24. They're in the search pattern when the Mi-24 spins, noses down and heads my way.

I fly down the other side of the ridge, on the edge of losing control. Near the bottom, the inevitable happens, and the jeep high sides on a boulder, tossing me out. I scramble out of the trees and groan.

It hurts to breathe. I check my rifle is functional and hobble away from the jeep. To my left is the river delta, on my right scant woods for cover and concealment.

To my surprise the Mi-24 lands and six Spetsnaz troopers jump out.

An RPG rocket screams by the helicopter, and it lifts off and flies away. I take two soldiers with my suppressed rifle before the rest of the squad knows what's happening. I turn and hobble in the direction the RPG came from.

I'm sweating, rasping for air. I trip and scramble up. Rounds tear up the trees. I spin on my knees and catch another soldier with a quick burst. I take a round in the left shoulder.

It spins me to the ground. My hand comes away dark red. I want to stop and tend to it. My eyes are watering. I blink and take deep breaths to focus.

The blood flow demands attention, but I don't have the time. I scuttle to a tree and pull out a grenade. I use the front sight of the rifle to pull the pin.

I scream a war cry and toss it toward the three remaining Spetsnaz troopers. When it detonates, I'm up and running. Rounds go by in an unaimed spray. I sense a helicopter and scan the sky.

Bad day, getting worse. It's the Mi-8 troop carrier. Another RPG flies through the sky and strikes it in the landing gear. It leaves the area. But the Mi-24, swoops down the face of the ridge, its nose gun blazing at an unseen target.

The remaining Spetsnaz soldiers are keeping their rate of fire up as they follow me. They are not conscripts, they're pros. I stop and heave my last grenade.

There's a cry. I'm running out of air as my legs churn and my arms pump. I've got to find the people with the RPG. A third RPG streaks by and impacts metal from the sound of it.

Bullets fill the air. I keep running. I can't look.

I pick up the sound of a different helicopter.

A bullet strikes my right calf and I tumble into the open.

I can't stop. Grunting, I crawl for cover.

A machine gun lets off a long burst.

I shoot at the soldiers and run dry. I pull my pistol and take a shot before it jams. I'm working the problem when I'm yanked up right.

"Run for the helicopter, Wolf," Gates said and pushed me.

My run is more like a skip and hopping mess. There's a helicopter skimming the earth toward me. Behind me, Gates is burning through his belt of ammunition.

The helicopter is a Vietnam era Huey. It skids to me, and I scuttle in.

The lone pilot hands me an AK. I fire to cover Gates. The pilot slides the helicopter closer to his location. I dump a magazine of rounds at the soldiers as Gates flops onboard.

The pilot spins one-eighty and takes off for Georgia. We struggle into the seats and strap in with our backs to the pilot.

Gates is assessing my wounds. I turn my head to the pilot. "Thanks brother, much appreciated."

"Don't thank me," the pilot says without taking his eyes off the terrain. "Thank the colonel."

We're flying ten feet off the ground, bobbing and weaving over farmland and into streams and riverbeds. I'm not sure when we crossed the border. My eyes are closed.

I'm sweating in the cool air, and I might vomit all over this old war bird. I told Gates no morphine and I'm regretting it. I feel the helicopter gain altitude and reduce airspeed. I'm scanning the air for the Mi-24.

"We're good, Wolf. We're in Georgian airspace," Gates said.

"Outstanding," I say. It's all I can muster.

Gates is smiling and it's infectious. I'm smiling and cough out a laugh. It hurts.

"Your brother is one heck of a pilot."

It's an odd statement considering what we went through. "Yes, sir. I'm sure he is."

Now Gates is laughing. "What is it, sir?"

The colonel is gesturing to the pilot. His visor is up now. It hurts to rotate my head, and I squint.

It takes a beat and I try and jump up, but the seat belt keeps me in place. I groan, my vision blurs, but I don't care. My stepbrother Bjorn is the pilot.

I spend the next couple of weeks as a visitor in the secure ward at Fort Bragg's Womack Army Medical Center.

I've got twelve years in the Army. I've done everything I wanted to do. I walk when the nurses let me, and I ponder what I want more? To be a Special Forces team sergeant or to go deeper into the technology I know is coming out of the intelligence community.

If I stay in the Army, I'll be promoted to E-8, Master Sergeant. But it will require my reenlisting for another three years. I'll be assigned a team and if I stay five to six more years I can retire as a Command Sergeant Major.

If I go contractor, I'll at least double my salary. I can build a good life, have a family. I'll be living the American dream. I'll still be in the fight, but twice removed.

Unless I transfer to one of the National Guard Special Forces units. I've worked with the 20th before. Good guys. They all hold jobs and continue to serve their country.

If I stay in, I'll receive full retirement and all the other benefits of twenty years' service. But the opportunity cost is high. Several tens of thousands of dollars towards a degree and building out the life I want to live.

They are letting me walk more, and this is all I think about. I'm deliberate when I plan for the future but to be honest, I have been lucky.

Volunteering has worked out well. Except for this last quote, training event.

Three days before I'm due to be released, I hear from Kennedy. I've kept in touch with him, and he's sent me a contractor job posting at US Special Operations Command.

He thinks I'm a perfect fit, and I tend to agree. I'll still be part of the team, but not running for my life.

Gates and Morgan think it's a good idea. Gates is getting promoted to full colonel and will be at SOCOM as the National Guard advisor. He's excited and will start my transfer to 3rd Battalion 20th Special Forces Group. He's also connecting me with a realtor friend to talk Tampa housing.

I tell the colonel thanks, but I need to land the job first. I hobble to the learning center and create a resume. I have Kennedy edit it before I email it to the recruiter via my Hotmail account. I'm surprised when I receive a call the next day. The recruiter is interested in me and he's tracked me to the hospital.

The day after I'm released, I'm on a plane to Tampa. I talk with five people in a day, and I'm surprised how we bond over tech and shared military experience. I like the team and the company culture. I spend another day with the realtor looking at townhouses and appreciate the lower cost for everything.

The job offer comes through, and I'm happy for a new chapter in my life. I accept via phone call and will sign the offer, which is on its way FedEx for delivery tomorrow. I call my parents, and my mom, as usual, puts Andy and herself on speaker. I tell them about the job offer and my acceptance. They are excited for me.

"How was your trip, Lance?" Mom asked.

"Good, good. Fell off a bike and got dinged up a little, but good."

"No more getting dinged up in this new job?"

"Not unless a retiree runs over me," I say and laugh. "I'm buying a townhouse in Tampa. I'll call you with the details after I take possession."

"We are proud of you, Lance. Serving you country, buying a house. Are you thinking about starting a family?" Mom asked.

"Yes, Mom, I am. But I'm going to take my time to ensure I find the right person. Don't worry though, you'll see grandkids soon enough."

"Lance Bear Wolf, you better keep your word!"

We all laugh, and I say goodbye. Now I'm focused on my new job and making an impact.

CHAPTER
THIRTY-EIGHT

OCTOBER 1998

Work is great. I like the people and the mission focus. In the US Special Operations Command intelligence division where I work, we have the latest intelligence platforms and systems at our disposal. I'm being read onto new programs and technology monthly.

The Tampa area and Florida are more to my liking than I suspected they would be. My 20th Special Forces Group team is solid. I've made friends with training sites and options, which include Mike Boats and other cool stuff most guard units never get to experience.

We've already deployed to Tolemaida once, and I'm talking with the operations division here at the command about supporting 2nd Battalion, 7th Group during its training rotation with Mexican Special Forces.

On my weekly call with my parents, they surprise me.

"A buddy called asking for help. We're headed to Puerto Vallarta for four months in November. He's got a deep-sea fishing charter," Andy said.

"I'm happy for you guys," I say, thinking how long it has been since I enjoyed their company. "I might be able to get some time off. If it works out, do you mind if I join you?" I ask.

My mother brakes cover and yells an ancient cry welcoming a warrior home.

"I'll let you know if I can join you," I say and disconnect.

Odd how the spirits have lined up the potential to spend time with my parents with my need to hurt the cartels.

Life and death.

I just hope I can keep them separate.

The End.

ACKNOWLEDGMENTS

This novella along with my two books in the Shadow Tier series are only possible through the loving pushes and straight forward feedback of my biggest supporter, my wife.

In no particular order, I'd like to acknowledge the following authors and readers who keep me excited about the stories I tell and the characters I bring to life.

The Silverback Publishing team and *James Abt* in particular, for keeping me on track. To *Ama Adair* for moderating and generating topics and questions for our discussions with some of the best authors in the Thriller genre.

A.J. Tata, Mike Bennett, Don Bentley, Jeff Wilson, and Brian Andrews, thank you for joining me to discuss the impact the military had on us personally and our writing. These gentlemen have been invaluable supporters and continue to show me the way to better my craft and understanding of the publishing industry.

My Beta readers, *Mark Elliot, Steve Netter, the BTB team,* and the Stratton/Pope family led by the boss, my wife…like they had a choice.

Mark Sibley, Mike Bennett, Adam Sikes, Eric Bishop, Jeff Circle – your read of the ARC was invaluable.

To all the people that pre-ordered the novella, thank you! I appreciate your support and getting the word out. Shout out to *Brian Simmons,* the first to preorder.

I can't let this page be finished without mentioning my ITW critique partners; *Millie Hast, Jack Stewart, Brian Godden, Traci Abramson, Alan Spira, Ann Feinstein, and Dave Elliott.* They push and encourage me to become a better writer every day.

This year I've been able to join many top podcasters on their shows and I can't thank them enough. *Dave Temple host of The Thriller Zone, JM Guarnieri host of Spear Talk, Jeff Clark host of Course of Action,* and too many others to list.

While unrelated to the novella, I want shout out a big THANK YOU to *David Temple* for bringing Lance Bear Wolf and the Shadow tier team to life in the Shadow Sanction audiobook.

2024 is starting off with a bang and I'm excited for what's next. Stay tuned to Steve's Squibs for information on Book 3 in the Shadow Tier series and more.

To the past and future men and women of the US Army Special Forces Regiment

#DOL De Oppresso Liber - Free the Oppressed!

ABOUT THE AUTHOR

Steve Stratton started his military career at the White House Communications Agency supporting the needs of President's Ford and Carter, Vice President's Rockefeller and Mondale and Secretary of State Henry Kissinger. He transitioned to the US Secret Service but after several years and an election campaign, Steve left for the commercial sector.

Steve was awarded his Green Beret in 1986. From the 80's through 2000 he deployed with 20th Special Forces on counter-drug and training missions in the SOUTHCOM region. His civilian contractor time includes support for USCENTCOM, USSOCOM, and several intelligence agencies. Today he advises cybersecurity vendors that support the warfighter and intelligence community. When he is not working, You can find him mountain biking, trout fishing, or hunting in Colorado.

ALSO BY STEVE STRATTON

Shadow Tier

Shadow Sanction

Lance Bear Wolf #4 - Fall 2024